# "Speak to the Earth"

## a novel

## William Bell

SEAL BOOKS

Seal Books and colophon are trademarks of
Random House of Canada Limited.

SPEAK TO THE EARTH
Seal Books/published by arrangement with Doubleday Canada
Doubleday Canada edition published 1994
Seal Books edition published 1996

ISBN 0-7704-2724-3

Cover art copyright © Ron Lightburn

*Although this book was inspired by actual events,
it is a work of fiction. Any resemblance between my
characters and real persons, living or dead, is coincidental.*

Seal Books are published by
Random House of Canada Limited.
"Seal Books" and the portrayal of a seal are the property of
Random House of Canada Limited.

Visit Random House of Canada Limited's website:
www.randomhouse.ca

PRINTED AND BOUND IN THE USA

OPM 10 9 8 7 6 5 4 3 2 1

This book is dedicated to the memory of my uncle

Thomas Spowart

*Speak to the earth, and it shall teach thee.*

— Job 12:8

# OVERTURE:

# The
# Badlands

He was born in a ditch, and he spent the first ten years of his life among secrets and bones.

In the tourist brochures the land is described differently. An hour and a half northeast of Calgary, Highway 9 pushes across the rolling Alberta prairie under a phenomenon of sky. The green expanse on either side of the two-lane blacktop is patched with immense and dazzling oblongs of brilliant yellow rapeseed or purple-blue alfalfa. In that place, an eternity of wind presides.

Suddenly, there opens before the eye a deep canyon. A sharp descent between ramparts of grey-brown earth cuts off the horizon and leads to one of the most fascinating geological formations in the great plains of North America. Bryan called it a ditch.

Long ago, as countless centuries crept by, the Alberta Badlands were gouged into the prairie by retreating ice fields, scraped by punishing winds and eroded by the swift current of the Red Deer River. The steep irregular walls of the canyon, gutted and creased, are composed of rock, clay and sand that crumble to the touch; and in their slow decay they yield a treasure of fossils unequalled anywhere on earth. A lot of people, Bryan often mused, seemed excited by this fact.

His home town, Drumheller, Alberta, was famous for two things, both of them related to fossils. The rich seams of coal that had appeared inexhaustible to generations of miners and their families had played out long before Bryan was born, leaving slag heaps and burned-out caverns. More dramatic were the remains of numerous species of dinosaurs that had disappeared under mysterious and hotly debated circumstances. Whatever the secret of their extinction, they must in the days when they lumbered, slithered and ran through what were then tropical swamps and grasslands, have seemed masters of a world that would continue forever.

To Bryan, it seemed that every building in his home town and along the Dinosaur Highway sported the image of a saurian: the T-Rex Café, the Brontosaurus Motel, the Dinosaur Children's Park. He lived, with his mother and father, above the Albertosaurus Stop 'n Shop, a convenience store attached to a discount gas station. While the other kids searched pointlessly for something interesting to do in Drumheller, Bryan pumped gas, cleaned windshields, gave directions to tourists and wished he didn't live in a community where all the interesting things had occurred millions of years ago.

The Troupe family business made money in the summer — when the valley was flooded with waves of tourists gawking at the "hoo-doos" down the road or crowding into the Royal Tyrell Dinosaur Museum up the road — and lost it all again in the winter, when the waves became barely noticeable ripples. So, while Iris managed the store and the gas pumps, Norm, a resourceful mechanic, found work in the oil fields. Bryan was under strict instructions to keep quiet about his mother's ongoing battles with creditors and suppliers. "Your dad's got enough to worry about," she would say. When Norm was home he and Bryan put in many happy greasy hours assembling an old Harley-Davidson Electra Glide that Norm had bought in a box when Bryan started first grade.

One spring, when Bryan was ten, Iris got a phone call from northern Alberta. Norm had been working on a donkey rig when a cable snapped and struck him, splitting his safety helmet with the force of the recoil. Iris had to go up north and bring her husband back home in a plywood coffin. Two days later Norm's bones were laid beside his parents' in the Baptist cemetery in Drumheller.

Not long afterwards, Bryan came home from school to find his mother sitting behind the counter in the store, crying, an open letter in her trembling hands. Gently, Bryan pried the page from her fingers and read that his dad had left him and his mother two hundred thousand dollars from an insurance policy.

"No wonder the crazy bugger never had any money," she wept. "He was saving it all for us."

On his last day of school that year Iris told her son that she wanted to go back to British Columbia. She couldn't stand Drumheller without Norm, she said. She wanted to sell out and go home. Her brother Jimmy would take them in. What did Bryan think?

"Do they have trees there?" he asked.

Iris laughed for the first time since the funeral. "I'm pretty sure they do."

"Then let's go."

Three weeks later Bryan and his mother loaded up the Harley and pointed it west.

Bryan enjoyed riding pillion behind his mother, watching the prairie roll by as the Harley purred along the blacktop. Once past Calgary and the foothills, they were embraced by the shadows and mists of the Rockies. They rumbled through passes, along the banks of foaming rivers, powered up slopes streaked and patched by sun, twisted through Rogers Pass and made a camp outside of Kamloops.

They rode into Vancouver the following afternoon and caught the ferry to Vancouver Island. About twenty minutes outside Port Albert, the highway took a long curving climb up the side of a mountain. At the summit, Iris kicked down through the gears and pulled off the road. Bryan dismounted and shook the stiffness out of his legs as his mother leaned the cycle on its stand, shut it down and climbed off.

Before them lay a valley and the mountains beyond, a rolling sea of green, patched with moving shadows cast by clouds that sailed peacefully across the blue sky. The light breeze carried the scent of the forest. From the bush along the road, birdsong trickled. It was, Bryan thought, nice. As different from the arid Badlands as it could possibly be. The scene calmed him, and for the first time since he had left home he felt glad that he was going to live here.

Iris groaned. "Look what they've done."

"What? What's the matter, Mom?"

Iris pointed across the valley. "The loggers."

"I don't see anyone."

Then Bryan realized what she meant, and his exhilaration crashed. What he had thought were shadows on the mountains were gigantic treeless scars, some of them hundreds of hectares in size, as if some malignant disease had stripped the slopes to the bone. The loggers had left nothing standing. The ground was choked with branches, snags and bark, pierced by thousands of blackened, skeletal trunks.

"That's clear-cut logging," Iris said. "It wrecks the ecosystem. See that road?"

Through one of the blank areas a road had been cut into the side of the hill, and from it irregular trenches snaked down the hillside, gouged into the mountain by wind and rain.

"Yeah."

"Because there's no vegetation left to hold the soil,

erosion and mud slides carry the topsoil down to the foot of the mountain and clog the streams. That destroys the spawning beds." She sighed. "Jimmy told me in his letter that things would look different from the way they did when I left the island, but I didn't imagine this. He said that near Quesnel there's a clear-cut that's fifty kilometres long. It's a bloody abomination, isn't it?"

"You mean the whole island is like this?"

"No, thank God. Let's get the hell out of here."

It was evening when Bryan and his mother pulled into Nootka Harbour, the fishing village on the Pacific coast where Iris had grown up. They found Jimmy's house easily — a bungalow perched on the rocky shore well above the surf. Silence rushed in around them when the Harley's motor died, and the air was heavy with a delicious brew of strange odours. Bryan would someday be able to identify: fragrances of the sea, the forests and time. They dismounted, stiff and sore. Jimmy wasn't at home, but he had left the door unlocked and a welcome note on the kitchen table, printed in pencil on a piece torn from a paper bag. Bryan helped his mother unpack the Harley and push it out of the way under the car port.

The next day Bryan drained the oil, replaced it, bled the gas tank and fuel lines, threw a tarp over the Harley, and never looked at it again.

# PART ONE:

# Spring

# ONE

After she had passed out the tests, Mrs Richmond sat at her desk and crossed her arms over her bony chest. "All right," she cackled cheerily, "you may begin."

Bryan took a look at the test paper. Oh, oh. She couldn't have, he thought. The witch.

The night before, Elias had come over to study, bringing a few CDs, a bag of corn chips, but no books. Typical. "We'll use yours," he had told Bryan. The two of them had watched TV for an hour or so, until Iris chased them to Bryan's room. He had made the mistake of telling his mother about the big test coming up.

"Richmond gave us three questions a week ago. One of them will be the test, and we don't find out which one until tomorrow."

"In other words, she wants you to prepare three good answers."

"Right," Elias put in. "She figures to get three for the price of one. But Bry and I are going to fool her."

Iris stood in the doorway, hands on her hips. She

curled her hair around the end of one finger as she spoke. "Let's see the questions."

Bryan handed her the question sheet. "It'll be number one," she said after she had perused the paper. "Take my word for it. But, to be sure, you should get ready for all of them."

"Nah," Bryan said. "She'll want to squeeze us on something new. There's no way she'll give us the first question. We already did a project on it."

"You mean the one you failed," Elias added from Bryan's bed, where he sprawled comfortably, two pillows behind his head and the bag of corn chips open on his chest. Bryan was Elias's best friend, but that didn't spare him from the sarcasm for which Elias was famous. Elias was the same age as Bryan — fifteen — and the two had been friends since Bryan and Iris had come to Nootka Harbour. His dad was a Coast Salish artist who operated a gallery in their home, and his Anglo mom was a writer whose poems were often printed in the local paper. Elias himself liked to write songs and pick out tunes for them on his old Yamaha guitar.

"Yeah," Bryan admitted, "the one I failed. Let's get to work on two and three, if you can tear yourself away from those corn chips."

"You're making a mistake," Iris warned as she walked down the hall to the kitchen.

Bryan hated it when his mother was right. Now, here on the exam paper, was the question he and Elias had confidently decided not to prepare. *In a two-page essay, compare the importance of the forestry industry to the fishery with respect to the economy of British Columbia.* He caught sight of Elias, two rows over, giving Bryan his famous I-told-you-so look. Bryan shrugged and rolled his eyes. Elias pantomimed a strangulation.

Fish, rocks and trees. That's B.C., Bryan mused, at least here on Vancouver Island. Thank goodness I don't have to write about mining. Trees and fish. Okay, trees and fish.

He looked out the window, which was, as usual, being hosed down by spring rain, then at Mrs Richmond, whom Bryan wished he could have hosed down with sulphuric acid until she dissolved into a thin column of smoke and a pile of empty clothing, like the Wicked Witch of the West. She sat unperturbed behind her desk, scanning the room for cheaters.

Staring at the empty foolscap where his answer should have been forming itself by now, Bryan clicked his ballpoint a couple of times. He inked in the *o* in "forestry" and the *e* in "fishery." No profound thoughts came to mind. He sighed and began to write in large round letters.

*British Columbia is a beautiful province and since my mother and I moved here about five years ago, it has been my home. We are lucky to live in such a beautiful place.*

He paused and looked at the ceiling for inspiration, then balled up the paper, earning a scowl from Mrs Richmond for shattering the scholarly silence of the room. It's a good name for you, you old bat, he thought.

W-cubed. The Wicked Witch of the West.

All around him kids scribbled industriously. *Question Number One*, he printed on the top of a new sheet of foolscap — a pretty redundant move, since the exam had only one question. Leaving two empty lines, he began in the same oversized writing. *Some say the forestry is the most important industry in British Columbia. It's true that trees are really really important to the people and the economy of our beautiful province.* He paused and looked out at the rain again. *After all, where would we be without them?* Reading over this brilliant introduction, he added, *The trees, that is, not the people. Although people are certainly really really important too.* With a half-line indentation he began a new paragraph.

*Others, however, hold the opinion that the fishery is the main industry, because we have so many fish here, all over the place, and so many kinds. Like salmon and mackerel, to name only two. Of many. There is absolutely no question, that the fishery is really really crucial to the economy of our wonderful province of British Columbia, Canada. After all, where would we be without all those really really nice fish?*

Bryan had now completed slightly more than half a page of monster writing. He clicked his pen some more. *The question is, who is right? The forestry people or the fishery people?* I'll be damned if I know, he thought, wondering how he was going to fill two whole pages.

No amount of fertilizer shovelled onto the page would induce W-cubed to cough up marks unless there were a few facts mixed in. Richmond was a "counter":

she hunted for facts she had taught the class and, when she ran into one, flagged it with a red check mark. Bryan searched his limited memory for anything Iris or Jimmy might have said that W-cubed might consider worthy of a red mark.

His uncle had laboured all his life as a logger, wherever he could find work. In Oregon, the interior of B.C. and here on the island he had felled trees. Iris's knowledge about resource industries was less direct: nevertheless, she clung tenaciously to many opinions about fishing and logging — often much to her brother's annoyance. She complained regularly that the fishery would eventually die out, just as the cod stocks had on the East Coast. "And they've polluted the ocean so badly that the fish will all be poisoned to death if we — or the Japanese trawlers — don't net them first. With Vancouver dumping minimally treated sewage into the gulf, it's a wonder the bloody salmon can make it to the Fraser, let alone up the Fraser. They had to shut down the shellfish industry last year because the stuff isn't fit to eat. And the forests," she railed, "don't even talk to me about the clear-cuts."

"I won't, don't worry," Jimmy had put in. "I'd hate to slow down your tirade with a bunch of facts."

Undeterred, Iris had finished up with a monologue about the depleted ozone layer.

But Bryan couldn't remember anything from his mother's rants or his uncle's arguments that would help him now. He fixed his eyes on the source of his pains. To

Bryan she resembled a bespectacled stick wrapped in brown tweed. He wondered how on earth she had ever become a Mrs. Then, inspiration struck. He remembered that Mr Richmond was a local manager for MFI — Mackenzie Forest Industries.

Quickly, in almost normal-sized writing, he scribbled, *In the economy of British Columbia, the forest industry is our best friend.* . . .

Bryan could not remember when his biological alarm clock had jangled his hormones awake and sent them singing through his blood. As he stumbled through puberty they crooned secret messages, then shrieked abrupt and startling commands, and finally staged a full-scale demented opera in his body that often left him exhausted and confused.

The Health classes at school, with their clinical talk about gonads, body hair and breasts, offered explanations but little understanding or comfort. All Bryan knew for sure was that somewhere between grade five and now, girls had miraculously transformed themselves from boring, noisy and essentially stupid creatures to graceful and alluring beings whose clothing fit them a lot better than it used to. And since her arrival at Talbot Inlet Junior High last September, the female who most commanded his attention was Ellen Thomson.

She was in his class, and sat three rows over and two ahead. When she raised her hand, her shirt would stretch tightly across her breasts. Her thick red hair, usually worn in a French braid, swayed softly across her back when she moved her head, or fell forward when she bent over her work.

"You stare at her butt much harder and you'll burn a hole through her jeans," Elias had once said as they lined up in the cafeteria for french fries.

"Shut up, Elias. I wasn't staring."

"As if. Not that I blame you. She's got one of the nicest rear ends in this pitiful excuse for a school."

"She's not just a body, you know."

"Yeah, sure."

Elias had, as he so often did, struck Bryan in a sensitive spot. When his hormones wailed at him he felt guilty thinking about Ellen that way. He knew he should be drawn to her personality, her mind, her accomplishments — she was an A-student and a star athlete — but how could he be attracted to her character when she was a stranger? He knew more about her green eyes, the curve of her brows and the spray of freckles across her nose than he did about her nature.

That day, after lunch, he confided his guilt to Elias, whose response was typical.

"Relax, Bry, you're normal. Besides, let's be honest. How many times does a guy look at a passing skirt and say, 'Hey! Nice personality!' or 'Check out the mind on that one!'"

"Thanks a lot, Elias. You're a big help."

Bryan envied his best friend, and sometimes he felt guilty about that, too. Elias could talk the talk, make the girls laugh, ask them out on dates. With his dark skin, jet-black hair and wide shoulders, he was a natural. He could make up funny songs and sing them under his breath in class, setting up ripples of laughter that circled around him and splashed across the room.

I, Bryan thought, am the opposite. Not short but not tall. Not ugly but not cute either — the stiff wavy ginger hair and pug nose I inherited from my dad guarantee that.

On the few occasions when he had tried to converse with a female of his own age, he'd rehearsed what he was going to say. Inside his head the words sounded pretty good. But when they came out of his mouth — garble. He felt like the only guy in the world who could trip over his own tongue.

The day of the disastrous test, Elias and Bryan were splashing across the school yard to board the school bus that took them home to Nootka Harbour, nine miles down the peninsula. The rain had let up, and the kids on the bus were even more boisterous than usual. As the two boys made their way back to the back of the bus, Elias stopped Bryan.

"Look," he said above the confusion of voices around them, pointing to an empty seat beside Ellen.

"No way," Bryan said.

"Okay, if you're too chicken."

As they passed Ellen Bryan found himself shoved into the seat beside her, his escape blocked by Elias's broad back as he began talking to a tall gawky girl named

Shirley. Bryan rose and shoved Elias, who stood as immovable as a Douglas fir. At that moment the bus lurched forward with an audible grinding of gears, knocking Bryan onto his rear again. He stared at the metal back of the seat in front of him. He gulped, aware that his heart had sped up alarmingly and that a hot flush crept up his neck and into his face.

"How did you do on the big test?"

"Uh, are you talking to me?"

Ellen smiled and tossed back her hair. "See anybody else in this seat?"

Bryan forced himself to face her. She was wearing tight blue jeans and an oversized red leather vest over a white T-shirt. He gulped again.

"Oh, uh, yeah, I guess you're right." What a smooth talker you are, Bryan, he thought to himself. By now she probably thinks you're retarded.

"So?"

"Uh . . . so . . . ?"

"The test. Do okay ?"

"Oh, yeah. I mean, no. Not really. I'm pretty sure I, you know, failed it." He found himself scratching his ear and quickly pulled his hand away. "How about you?"

"I did okay, I think. I studied a lot. I like school."

"Yeah, me too."

"No, you don't. You never take any books home and you flunked the last project."

Thanks to W-cubed, everyone in class had been treated to the spectacle of Bryan slinking to her desk and receiving his essay. Richmond had handled it as if it were a dead fish.

"Well, that's true. But I'm going to work hard now. I really am. I learned my lesson."

Ellen laughed. "Yeah, sure," she said. "I'm Ellen Thomson, by the way."

"I know. Hi. I'm Bryan Troupe."

"I know. I sort of know your mother."

"My mom? From where, the supermarket?" Bryan hoped not. Iris worked at the grocery store as a cashier. Ellen's parents were well off — her father was some kind of supervisor in MFI and her mother was a lawyer.

"No, I saw her at the school meeting a while ago. She made a pretty passionate speech."

"Really?" Bryan said, groaning inwardly. Bracing himself to make a quick exit, he looked to the aisle, but Elias was still there, his torso swaying with the movement of the bus.

"I was impressed," Ellen added.

Bryan expected but did not find a note of sarcasm in her voice. Forget this girl, he thought, suddenly angry at his mother, and not for the first time. A few months before, a small group of parents, led by the Thomsons, had tried to get a book banned from the school library because it was "sacrilegious." Something about witches or ghosts. Iris had gone to the meeting — probably in her grungy old pink track suit, Bryan thought.

"My parents made me go," Ellen told him. "One of the parents stood up and said the book didn't belong in a decent Christian community, especially a school, where it could corrupt young minds. Your mom told the group she was a Christian, too, and if their idea of Christianity was to ban harmless books just because their narrow little minds were offended, then they were way out of line. That's not democracy, she said."

"Mom can get pretty wound up about that stuff," Bryan said lamely. "Sometimes she gets out of line herself."

"Well, maybe."

Bryan sweated and racked his brains for a clever way to change the subject. He gave up. Ellen looked out the window. Well, that's it, Bryan, he thought, you blew your chance. Not that you ever really had one.

"Excuse me," Ellen said as the bus pulled up at the end of her lane. The big house she lived in was barely visible through the spruce trees that lined the road.

"Oh, uh, sorry." Bryan was relieved that she was leaving. The pressure was killing him. He stood in the aisle to let her pass.

"Anyway," she said, gathering up her books, "if you're serious about what you said, maybe we could study together some time." And with that she went down the aisle and out the door.

Bryan stood there with his mouth open, wondering if his ears were working properly, until the bus ground forward again.

Elias slid in beside him. "So, how'd it go?"

"It didn't," Bryan answered, still not believing his ears.

"Hey, Bry, you got to get moving, man. I can't do everything for you."

# TWO

Bryan was setting the kitchen table for dinner when his mother and uncle came in, laden with bags of groceries.

"Hey, Bry," Jimmy called out as he put down his bags.

"Hey, Jimmy. What's for supper, Mom? I'm starved."

"Dead rats and rotten salmon roe," Jimmy cut in, lighting up a cigarette with a big chrome-plated Zippo lighter.

"The guest rooms need to be made up, dear," Iris told Bryan. "We got some customers coming on the weekend."

It must be March, Bryan mused. The whale-watchers are back in town.

Soon after they moved to Nootka Harbour, Bryan's mother had put some of Norm's life insurance money together with the few dollars she had salvaged by selling the business in Drumheller and bought a bungalow on the rocky shore of Osprey Cove, on the west side of town. Her job at the grocery store didn't pay much and there didn't seem to be an abundance of career opportunities in Nootka Harbour for a grade ten dropout, so she decided to dip once again into what she still thought of as Norm's kitty and start up a business. That was when Bryan's home became Norm's Bed 'n Breakfast.

Iris Troupe was a slender energetic woman with dark intelligent eyes and a razor wit. Most of the time she gave minimal attention to her appearance beyond cleanliness and tidiness, having formed the opinion long ago that most men were afraid of smart, strong-willed women, and having vowed that she'd be damned if she would deck out her body and be placid. No one in range of her voice was ever in doubt about what Iris thought about an issue. Norm had admired her mind and her sense of humour — he had once told her that he found brainy women sexy — but guys like Norm, Iris knew, didn't come along too often, and rather than wait around for one, she had a life to live and a son to raise.

Both she and Bryan were grateful on more than one occasion that she did not have to raise Bryan alone: her brother Jimmy was what Iris called a godsend. When the bungalow became a B&B, it was Jimmy who had done the work, interpreting Iris's freehand plans and drawings. Bryan had helped — which meant standing around, holding things, fetching tools and getting in Jimmy's way as he sawed and hammered spruce studs or put up drywall, whistling country-western laments and smoking unfiltered cigarettes.

In his late thirties, Bryan's uncle was a small dark quick-tempered man with a body hardened by a lifetime of rugged work. In a world that still valued larger men in both the romantic and economic spheres, Jimmy Lormer compensated for his size by strength and mental toughness — an attitude that had pushed him into more than a few fights in his youth. Having left school long before he was qualified for any kind of diploma, he was aware that all he had to offer an employer was honesty and a day's work.

About a year ago Jimmy had moved in with them. He had been laid off by MFI and lost his house when he got too far behind in his mortgage. He had stained the siding on the bungalow, painted every room inside and found things to fix. Jimmy could not sit still. Bryan thought he was a workaholic until one night, when Jimmy was out at the hotel "blowing the suds off a few," Iris explained that he was too proud to sit around and live off somebody else.

"We're not somebody else. We're his relatives," Bryan had protested. "And he isn't living off us. He doesn't have a job right now."

"That's how he feels, though," Iris had answered. "He can't help it. He won't even let me lend him money. If he isn't working, he feels useless."

After a dinner of sausages and beans, and after Bryan had finished his chores, he sneaked into the kitchen, hoping Jimmy and his mother weren't within earshot. The nine-o'clock news was on TV, and Bryan could hear them in the family room arguing good-naturedly about a report on the B.C. government granting tree farm licences to multinational corporations. Bryan picked up the phone, held his breath, punched three numbers and paused.

He put the phone down, exhaling with an audible whoosh. Maybe a glass of milk first. No, he had to grab the chance while there was no one else in the kitchen. The last thing he wanted was an audience. Once again he ran over the dialogue he had composed in his mind. Then, remembering to breathe normally, he pressed the buttons that made up Ellen's number and clamped his eyes shut.

"Hello?"

"Oh, uh, hi. Um, I was just wondering if you were, you know, serious on the bus today? About studying together?"

"Who is this?"

"Oh, damn! I mean, hello, Mrs Thomson. Is Ellen there?"

"Who's calling, please?"

Remembering just in time that Iris had given the Thomsons a verbal beating at the parents' meeting, Bryan said, "It's a friend from school."

"One moment, please."

When Ellen came on the line, Bryan rushed ahead. "Hi, it's Bryan. I —"

"Oh, hi. How are you?"

"Fine. Um, I was wondering —"

"So, did you think about my suggestion?"

"Your —"

"You know. About studying together?"

Wondering how much studying anyone could get done with someone who wouldn't let him finish a sentence, Bryan tried again. "Yeah, that's why I —"

"How about tomorrow after school?"

"Sure. Um —"

"Great. See you then. Gotta go."

Bryan returned to his room and looked at himself in the mirror. "You smooth dude," he said to his image. Then he laughed.

# THREE

Like a gladiator of ancient times or a medieval knight errant Bryan Troupe prepared himself for battle. His armaments: soaps, creams and lotions; floss, brushes, swabs and his uncle's safety razor. The field: the tiny bathroom of the Troupe bungalow, pulsing with rock music from a portable radio. His foe: his body, which seemed anxious to betray him at every turn. If his vigil was not constant, white flakes might break loose from his scalp and snow his hair or speckle his shoulders; a booger might peek maliciously from a nostril; malodorous liquid would seep from his armpits; dirt would collect secretly under his fingernails and between his toes. Each morning before school Bryan conducted a desperate rearguard campaign against the temple of his own flesh. Never did he feel completely successful.

But this evening he was going to Ellen Thomson's for the first time and he planned to flog his enemy into total submission. In the shower, he turned slowly under a jet of scalding water. With a shampoo-conditioner that smelled like apples and peaches and guaranteed an end to dandruff, he washed his hair three times, then shut off the water. He soaped up a rough washcloth and, beginning at his hairline, vigorously punished his skin, pausing to assault his ears, advancing downwards to chafe his armpits, attack his crotch, buttocks, legs, and grind loose skin from the depressions in his feet and between his toes. Under the shower again, the foam slid off his body and swirled down the drain. Bryan repeated the process.

By the time he pulled back the shower curtain, he was as pink, overheated and squeaky-clean as he had ever been in his life. The steam in the bathroom was so thick he could barely see. With his damp palm he squeegeed a small circle on the mirror and examined his upper lip. Today was the day he would remove from there the few downy blond hairs that made him look like a kid. Besides, if he ever was lucky enough to kiss Ellen, he didn't want to tickle her.

Using Jimmy's shaving brush and mug, Bryan worked up enough lather to shave a camel and applied the thick, creamy soap to his skin. When he was finished, his mouth had disappeared, his nostrils were clogged, and he couldn't breathe. He sneezed, blowing foam all over the mirror, his chest and the vanity top. He took a deep breath and dragged the razor over his upper lip. In two modest strokes, he was done.

And there was a gash under his nostril leaking bright arterial blood.

"Damn!" He ripped a piece of toilet paper from the

roll and stuck it to the offending wound. Before the mirror again, Bryan inspected his nostrils and ear holes for foreign particles. Finding none, he plugged in the hair dryer and attempted to bring order to his thick ginger hair. By the time he had given up in disgust, he realized that he was sweating heavily. The temperature in the steamy bathroom must have touched forty degrees. Fifteen minutes later he stepped out of the shower again, chilled to the bone.

Bryan dabbed another bit of toilet paper on his wound, then extracted a metre of dental floss from the plastic container. Pulling back his lips like a crazed ape, he began to floss, jamming the minty thread between his teeth, working it back and forth and yanking it out again, occasionally flicking bits of food onto the mirror. He then brushed his teeth. Twice. He swirled mouthwash around, gargled and spat into the sink.

The last stage of the battle had been reached. Bryan pulled the cap off a bottle of deodorant and, raising his arm like a victorious warrior, pumped a spray of fragrant liquid into his hairy armpit. For good measure, he pumped again. The bottle emitted a light farting noise. It was empty.

"Damn!" said the knight for the second time. He sneaked into his mother's bedroom and searched among the few bottles and jars on her dresser until he found an anti-perspirant stick with a wildflower depicted on the front. He applied a thick layer to his unprotected armpit, added some to the sprayed side, added more to the first

side. He went into his room, flapping his arms to dry th
sticky varnish. Then he dressed, taking twenty minute
to create the impression that he had tossed on his cloth
ing on the way out the door. He took a long, deep breath
and wished himself luck.

As Bryan left the house, Jimmy yelled, "Lookin
good, nephew. She'll love ya. Especially the toilet paper
on your lip!"

# FOUR

When Bryan bounded into the kitchen for breakfast one Saturday morning a week or so later, Jimmy was dishing out three portions of his famous Eggs James — a concoction of scrambled eggs, onions and tomatoes that looked like a modern painting on the plate. Iris was pouring coffee.

"Mom," Bryan said as he took his seat, "could you do me a small tiny little favour?"

Iris gathered her hair together at the nape of her neck and clipped a plastic barrette around it. "Sure," she said, throwing her arms out wide. "But first you have to tell me how you like my new T-shirt."

On the front of her bright green shirt "ORCA SOUND RAINFOREST" was embossed in darker green on a white conifer.

"It's nice, Mom, except that the colours are a bit mixed up. Most of the trees around here are green. What's it all about?"

"A few of us around town have formed a committee

to try and convince the provincial government to declare Orca Sound a natural preserve. You know, so we can protect the old-growth rainforest. Some of the animals and plants here are unique in the world. Did you know that?"

"That's real nice, Mom. Now about —"

"I'd like to hear what the big logging companies like MFI will have to say about your committee," Jimmy said, his mouth full of eggs and toast.

"Who gives a damn *what* MFI thinks," Iris shot back.

"Um, before you guys start your daily argument, could I get any answer, Mom?"

Iris smiled. "Sorry. What's the favour?"

"Could you look over the essay I wrote for Richmond?"

"Ah, the I-failed-the-test-so-I-had-to-write-an-essay essay," Jimmy said.

"Uncle, you're going to be wearing these eggs if you don't watch it. And, yes, that's the essay. Anyway, Mom, can you check the spelling and grammar and stuff? Don't change any of the facts, even if you don't agree with them, okay? Richmond's husband works for MFI and she thinks the company walks on water."

"So does the company. Okay, leave it in the family room."

"Thanks, Mom."

The kitchen door banged open and Walter shambled in, kicked off his rubber boots, poured himself a coffee and sat down.

Walter was a Nootka who lived with an ancient Irish setter named Dog in a trailer next to Norm's Bed 'n Breakfast. Before Jimmy had moved in, Walter had done odd jobs for Iris — a convenient but embarrassing state of affairs because Walter would not let Iris pay him. He had adopted her and Bryan and there was nothing either of them could do about it.

"Eggs, Walter?" Jimmy asked, pushing the bowl in Walter's direction without waiting for a reply.

"Don't want to put you to no trouble."

"No trouble, old friend," Iris said.

The ritual now performed, Walter silently ate. Over second cups of coffee, as Jimmy filled the kitchen with cigarette smoke, Walter commented, "Got some tourists on board today."

In his late fifties, Walter had spent most of his life on the sea or in the bush, so that the skin on his craggy face and calloused hands was leathery and dark. He was tall, heavy and arthritic and, as Iris once said not unkindly, he moved in slow motion. Walter owned an old fishing boat, and when necessity caught him by the throat or when a spirit moved him, he would put to sea. Sometimes he would hire out as a water taxi, when people could find him; sometimes he trapped crabs until he had enough money for a while, then quit until it ran out; and sometimes, when the whales were migrating — in March and October especially — he'd take tourists out to see them.

"That's good," Iris said. "Nice day for it. Looking for

whales, are they?"

"Yep. Got six people this time."

Walter was a man with a profound belief in silence. It was not unusual for him to come into the house, sit down with Iris and watch TV for an hour, then say "Gotta be goin'" and shuffle out the door, those three words having been the sum total of his oral communication. Nor did he take a head-on run at a topic when he did have something to say.

A few minutes and several sips of coffee later he added, "Lotta work, six people."

"Sounds like you could use a little help today," Jimmy suggested, looking at Bryan, who sometimes helped Walter out when his arthritis stiffened his fingers so much it made handling and baiting the crab traps difficult.

Bryan took the hint. "I wouldn't mind going along, if you've got the room. I've never seen whales close up."

Walter nodded to no one in particular. "Always got room for my best crabber."

"Do you have room for two?"

Jimmy rolled his eyes and said to his sister, "Ain't romance wonderful?"

"Mind your own beeswax," Bryan said when Iris giggled.

"Pretty big boat," Walter said.

Bryan figured he was probably the only person in Nootka Harbour who had not, at some time of his or her life, taken a trip out into the deep blue waters of the sound to see the greys, humpbacks or orcas. On the interest scale, whales ranked up there with watching paint dry or taking a walk to White's General Store to try on gloves. Twice a year tourists flooded into town from across Canada, the U.S. and even from Europe, to study the leviathans migrating north or south.

Now, here he was, blinking in the late-morning sun as he helped Walter get his weather-beaten but well-cared-for boat ready for just such a trip, looking forward to a day on the water with Ellen. As the customers — three middle-aged German couples decked out in new parkas and matching watch caps and hiking boots — climbed on board, Ellen swooped onto the dock on her mountain bike, dismounted, and locked it to the lamp post. Bryan introduced her to Walter, who grunted a greeting and fired up the diesel.

"Friendly," Ellen commented.

"You have to get used to him."

"I guess."

Walter piloted the boat up Gray's Passage and into the channel between Vickers and Flower Pot islands. Mount Vickers rose high above the rainforest, one side shadowed, the other lit up by the sun. Off the northernmost point of Flower Pot, an osprey floated high above the waves, scribing serene and watchful circles. Abruptly it pulled in its wings and dropped like a spear to the surf, sending up a puff of spray and, a few seconds later, beating its wings hard as it struggled into the air with a fish flopping in its talons.

The tourists stood at the rail in the bow, chattering and fussing with their cameras. The sun glinted off a flask that occasionally passed among them. In the stern, Bryan sat beside Ellen. Her green eyes sparkled and her red hair lifted and fell with the cool breeze. He put his arm around her and pulled her close.

Since that first evening, when he had gone to her house to study, terrified that he would betray himself with a stupid remark or trip over his own feet, he had seen her almost every night. Before his fourth visit to her house he had spent the day psyching himself up, for he had made up his mind to kiss her. I don't care if she tells me to get permanently lost, he had insisted to himself, I'm going to do it. Enough of this reserved scholarly crap.

All through the evening, as they pored over books and quizzed each other for an upcoming science test, he had chanted in the back of his mind, "I'm going to do it. I'm going to do it." When the quizzing was over and they were packing up the books in preparation for some serious video gazing, the chant had increased in intensity and the words had changed. "Now's the time. Now's the time."

He had sat down on the couch and readied himself for the attack while Ellen slid the movie into the VCR. "Okay," Bryan had told himself. "This is it. This is it." And as Ellen had traversed the rug that covered the patch of floor between them, "Don't wimp out. Don't wimp out." The timing would have to be perfect. Split second. As soon as she sat down, he would turn to her and plant a big one right on her gorgeous lips.

Here she was. He took a breath.

But she didn't sit down. In one startling motion she dropped to her knees beside him, put a firm hand on each of his shoulders, pushed him against the back of the couch and nailed him with a kiss that knocked his head back. Then, before he could react, she hit him with another, lingering this time.

"I got tired of waiting," she said as he caught his breath. "The suspense was killing me."

Once clear of the channel, the boat was gently lifted and lowered by the swells as it pushed out into Orca Sound. Bryan and Ellen brewed coffee on a small naphtha stove in the cramped cabin. As they passed out the steaming mugs to the tourists, a big blond man asked Bryan in a thick accent where the whales were.

"Don't worry," he said. "If anybody can find them, Walter can."

The man looked displeased. He poured something from the flask into his coffee. "I hope so. He is charging enough."

"Walter's the best."

"He'd better be."

Bryan returned to the stern, where Ellen had taken her seat again.

"I love this," she said. "I've spent hours watching the

orcas and belugas at the Stanley Park aquarium in Vancouver, but it just isn't the same as being out here. The whales are so amazing. They migrate about eight thousand kilometres a year."

"You mean eight *hundred*, don't you?"

"Nope. Thousand. The humpbacks winter around the Hawaiian Islands and the greys go down to Baja California. The calves are born in the warmer water. Then they come back to the North Pacific every spring. The humpbacks' round trip is about eight thousand klicks. I've been reading about them ever since I was a little kid. There aren't many of them left."

"You're beginning to sound like my mother."

"Huh?"

"Flukes," Walter called out casually, over the drone of the diesel. He pointed west and turned the wheel.

Bryan felt Ellen's body tense just before she jumped up and ran to the rail, peering ahead. "There they are!"

Bryan inched carefully along the gunwales and found a place at the rail beside her. The tourists were all shouting at once, pointing, aiming their cameras.

Bryan found it difficult to maintain his feeling of boredom; the excitement of the Germans, and especially of Ellen, was infectious. He scanned the undulating ocean ahead. About five hundred metres off the bow he saw white flashes in the surf. He suddenly realized they were not whitecaps.

"That's the underside of the flukes you see," Ellen explained, her voice heavy with wonder. "Those whales are humpbacks."

"How can you tell?"

"From the white underside of the flukes. And from the blow. There!" She pointed to a whiff of white mist that puffed into the air above the dark water. "The humpback's blow is sort of bushy."

As the boat ploughed toward the herd, the tourists became more ecstatic — shouting, pounding each other on the back, laughing.

"They're turning this way," Walter announced above the din. He cut the throttle.

With the engine now silent, other sounds filled Bryan's ears — the wash at the bow of the boat as it lost its momentum, the irregular splash of the long gentle swells, the cry of a gull that had followed the boat from shore and the constant gabble of the tourists. This last noise he unconsciously tuned out as the mammals moved toward him.

The flashing of the flukes could not be seen now because the whales were coming head on. Their dorsal fins appeared and disappeared; their backs arched and submerged, revealing the humps between the dorsal and the head. The blows puffed into the air.

To Bryan the whales seemed powerful, free, unconcerned with a few humans floating in a wooden boat on the surface of their ocean. They could go anywhere, in any weather; all the seas of the world were their realm. They were intelligent, and they breathed air. How could he ever have thought they were uninteresting?

About fifty metres out, the whales turned gracefully and passed by. Bryan felt a sudden chill as one of the humpbacks maintained its course straight toward him, its massive bulk becoming more apparent with every metre of water it covered. The dark hump rose from the surface, water foaming around it, then the three-metre-wide flukes broke from the sea and lifted high above the swell before sinking slowly out of sight.

A few moments passed. Voices murmured near Bryan, but his attention remained fixed on the surface of the sea. His breathing was quick, his throat dry. He felt the rapid thud of his heart. And then, like a small island rising from the floor of the sea, a gigantic shape loomed from beneath the waves, a shape almost twenty metres long. The dorsal fin cut the surface and the mammoth back broke from the surf, water cascading from the dark skin. The humpback's two blow holes spouted water four metres high, spraying Bryan and filling the air with the fetid odour of fish. The white edges of the whale's long curved wing flashed in the sun as it slipped alongside, raising the wing as if to avoid rubbing it against the hull. Bryan caught sight of the humpback's eye, an eye that seemed to examine him. The beast's back arched and the flukes towered above Bryan, throwing a long shadow over the water. And slowly, the gargantuan shape sank beneath the dark blue swells.

Bryan became aware of human voices once again and looked around. The tourists continued to laugh, talk, click their cameras. A few moments later, about ten metres off the bow, the surface of the Pacific boiled and foamed, and the whale's head reared up.

"Skyhop," Walter said.

"He's taking a look at us," Ellen explained.

Silently Bryan stepped away from her and braced himself on the gunwale alongside the cabin, still captivated by what he saw. A few more moments passed. A hundred metres to port he caught sight of a blow and then a dorsal fin. The humpback was heading straight for him again. Out of the corner of his eye he saw the blond tourist moving toward him until he stood at Bryan's side, elbows out as he held a camera to his eye.

The whale came on. It sounded, reappeared. The camera motor whizzed and buzzed as the man shot his pictures. The whale gracefully turned, raising his wing once again. Bryan heard a shout from the bow, felt a stunning blow as the man turned abruptly, slamming his elbow into the side of Bryan's head. Bryan dropped to the deck and slid head-first into the ocean.

The storm of sensations that broke inside his skull — the searing pain in his temple, the bone-crushing grip of the icy water, the numbing rush of terror — seemed to arrive in slow motion. He felt himself sinking. He felt and heard an unidentifiable sound, distorted, like a stereo turned up too loud. The noise enveloped him. A growling. A squeal. A door opening on rusty hinges.

The spell dissipated and, thrashing in panic, Bryan broke the surface, coughing and spluttering. He fought for breath when a wave crashed over him and he went down again, pulled deeper by his sodden clothing, falling into an arena of reverberation. A long, mournful whine. A hollow growl. His chest vibrated with the power of the sound.

Then, despite his terror, he knew. It was the whales. The whales were singing.

He felt a light tug at the back of his neck. A sharp jerk. Above him, shapes wavered against the light. He came to the surface to see Walter with a long pole in his hands. Bryan was pulled through the freezing swells to the stern, and Walter and Ellen hauled him into the boat.

"I heard them," a voice said as he lay gasping on the deck. "I heard them."

Soon afterwards, Bryan sat shivering uncontrollably in the cabin, out of the wind, with a cup of scalding black coffee clutched in his chilly hands. His head ached and his ribs were sore. Walter had stripped off Bryan's wet clothing and wrapped him in a thick goosedown sleeping bag, then returned to the controls to steer the boat back to Nootka Harbour. The blond tourist had come in and offered to add to the coffee a splash of something from his flask as he muttered his apologies.

"I thought Walter was going to throw that fool overboard," Ellen said after the tourist had left the cabin.

"I heard him singing."

"That stupid guy?"

"No, the humpback."

"You look like you're in a trance, Bryan. Are you okay? Maybe it's hypothermia." Ellen took the mug from him and held his shaking hands in hers.

"Huh? Oh, no," Bryan answered through chattering teeth. "I mean, yeah. I'm fine. I'm okay. Did you hear him, Ellen?"

"No. But I've heard them on tape."

"It was weird, like he was talking to me. Like he was trying to tell me something."

"Try to keep warm." Ellen pressed the coffee back into his hands. "Drink it while it's hot."

"They're great, aren't they," he said. "They're so *big*!"

"Yeah. They're the dinosaurs of the deep."

Bryan thought of his old home town, the arid Badlands holding their secrets and fossils, the giant bones of extinct dinosaurs.

"I hope not," he said.

# FIVE

B.C.'S FOREST INDUSTRY
draft one
by Brian Troupe
for Mrs Richmond
a make-up assignment for failing my test

The forestry industry in our province is one of the richest and most important. The other two ~~being~~ are mining and fishing. The biggest logging company in B.C. is Mackenzie Forest Industries which like a few of the others is ~~an international~~ a multi-national company. That means it is not owned completely by Canadians. Most of the rights to log the province ~~has~~ have been sold to these corporations.

Our wood products go all over the world to make paper, newsprint, furniture and houses, to name a few. About 90 per cent of the wood is exported in raw form and manufactured somewhere else, so there aren't very many manufacturing jobs connected ~~with~~ to the forestry for Canadians. ~~There's~~ There are about 76,000,000 cubic metres of wood in B.C. (Or is it Canada?)

Ninety per cent of the trees cut in B.C. are clear-cut, even though many countries in Europe don't allow it. (I couldn't find out why.) This is a method where all the trees in the area are cut down, although not all of them are used. Clear-cutting is safe and efficient and saves the lumber company a lot of ~~bucks~~ money. (Time is money!) Many clear-cuts are about 400 hectares in size. After the trees the loggers want are taken away, the clear-cut is set on fire to burn away the slash and ~~crap stuff~~ refuse left behind and other plant life so the area can be replanted. The replanting is to produce more trees, and herbicides and pesticides are sprayed regularly, just like on a farm. A lot of this replanting does not work — about half of it. (But I couldn't find out why.)

Nowadays the lumber business is a lot more efficient than it used to be. For example the rate of logging in B.C. has doubled since the 1960's. A machine called a "theller bunger" (sp?) which cuts the trees at ground level and lifts them up can do the work of about 12 loggers. So it's harder to get a job as a logger these days.

About two thirds of Alberta's forests are planned to be cut down, but I'm not sure about here in B.C.

So as you can see, like I said on my test (which I failed) the forestry industry is important to our province.

### MY BIBLIOGRAPHY

I watched two videos, "The Nature of Things" with David Suzuki (my uncle says he's a troublemaker and my mom thinks he's a saint) and "The Forests and You" and made notes on them. They contradicted each other all over the place.

I used our social studies textbook.

Ellen gave me pamphlets she got from her dad called "Wise Use of the Land Base" (the pamphlet, not her dad) and "Maintaining Sustainable Development" which I didn't understand too well.

My mother corrected some grammar mistakes.

Elias helped me with my spelling.

My mother and my uncle Jimmy gave me a little bit of information and a whole lot of opinions which contradicted each other and which I didn't use.

# SIX

R ain.

Rain hissing on the rocks of Osprey Cove and soaking the ground under the drenched trees beside the house. Rain drumming on the roof of the bus on the way to school. Rain running down the window panes of the classrooms. Rain beating umbrellas, pelting raincoats, saturating jackets and sweaters, chilling flesh and bone. Rain on the roof at night. In the morning, more rain.

It poured all the next week. People became grumpy, waiting for a crack of brightness to appear in the cement sky. Cats and dogs kept out of the way of impatient feet. Store clerks snapped at customers. At Bryan's house, Uncle Jimmy thumped around the house, complaining about everything, frustrated at being unemployed and unable to occupy himself outside. Only Iris held an even temper when the downpour closed off the town from the sun and the world — another proof, thought Bryan testily, that she was not a normal human being.

Within the drenched and dreary walls of his school, Bryan developed a grudging admiration for Mrs Richmond. Friday, in Social Studies, W-cubed took tedium to a new and unexplored level; she dragged boredom into another dimension. As she droned on, he secretly got out his thesaurus and made a list of all the synonyms for the word boring. Ellen was engrossed in a novel she was holding behind her textbook, a rare act of rebellion on her part. Elias pretended to take notes but, Bryan knew, he was composing songs and doodling.

The rain hissed and hummed; the clock's hands crept around its face.

Freed at last by the bell, Bryan dashed for the bus with Ellen and Elias, dodging around puddles pocked by the downpour.

"Hey, got an idea," Elias announced when they had found seats. Bryan and Ellen sat together, with Elias across the aisle.

"Congratulations," said Bryan.

"Mom's going to Port Albert tomorrow to do a poetry reading at the public library, and me and her have to visit my gram in the old folks' home. Why don't you two come with us? We can all hang around downtown for the morning while Mom is putting her audience to sleep, and you guys can do whatever until Mom and me are ready to go home."

"Sounds great," Ellen said. "Bryan and I can catch a movie."

"I don't know. I should probably help Walter tomorrow. He has a whale watch."

"Come on, Bryan," Ellen pleaded. "Walter can get along without you."

"I don't know."

"Well" — Elias gave Ellen a broad stage wink — "me and you can go without him."

"I'll be there," Bryan said.

At eight sharp the next morning, Bryan heard the rumble of the Wilsons' van in the driveway. Outside, the sky was sullen but at least the rain had stopped. He pulled on his hightops, slipped into his imitation suede bomber jacket and sang out a goodbye to his mother and uncle. Bryan climbed into the back seat of the van, which smelled of new wood, paint and linseed oil. Elias's father used it to transport supplies and finished canvases.

It took only a few minutes to drive across town to Ellen's. Mrs Wilson beeped the horn, which was, Bryan thought, totally unnecessary because anyone not deaf would know they had arrived.

"What's new, Bryan?" Mrs Wilson asked. "We haven't see you around our place much lately."

"The reason why," Elias cut in, "just came out her front door."

"Oh, not much, Mrs Wilson," Bryan replied. "Mom's joined that new park committee. Jimmy's still looking for work."

"It's pretty grim out there, all right," she said as Ellen got into the van. She sat next to Bryan, who immediately lost interest in making small talk with Elias's mother.

Once past Talbot Inlet, Highway 93 twisted and turned through the mountainous terrain. Elias's mother drove slowly and carefully, especially when caught behind one of the many logging trucks that carried timber in to the pulp mills and sawmills of Port Albert.

"Hey, Ellen, got that new tape you told me about?" Elias asked.

Ellen handed an Icicle Invasion tape to Elias, who jammed it into the deck and turned up the volume. Mrs Wilson immediately adjusted it to a reasonable level.

"Good stuff, eh?" Ellen commented, swaying to the pulsing bass.

Elias was turned around in his seat, facing Ellen and Bryan. Mostly Ellen, Bryan thought. When had they talked about the tape? he wondered.

"Heard this one yet, Bry?" Elias asked.

"He's been too busy reading about whales," Ellen answered for him, smiling. "He's becoming an expert."

"He'd better move fast," Mrs Wilson said as she floored the gas pedal and moved around a slow-moving lumber truck, "before they're extinct."

"Has he tried to talk to them again?" Elias joked.

"No, but I think he's working up to it."

Bryan looked out the window at the mountains, with their clear-cut bald spots. He worried when Elias and Ellen were together, especially if he wasn't with them. Not that Elias would try to steal Ellen away from him, Bryan reassured himself. But Elias didn't have to try. Whenever he was around a girl, you might as well stand back and shut up, because whoever the girl was, Elias was all she saw. There was no use trying to compete with him. There were times when he wished Ellen wasn't so good-looking.

At length they reached town, and Mrs Wilson deposited Elias, Ellen and Bryan on the main street.

"Good luck in your reading, Mrs Wilson," Ellen called out.

"Luck, Mom. Bye!" Elias yelled as the van rumbled away from the curb. "Whew! Smells like the pulp mills are going full tilt," he said, sniffing the damp air. The sulphurous odour hung in the air like invisible fog.

Bryan and his friends spent the morning window-shopping and exploring the music stores. Bryan moped along while Elias entertained Ellen with jokes and silly antics and she, it seemed to Bryan, laughed hysterically at every word that came out of Elias's mouth. They ate slabs of lukewarm pizza at a waterfront joint on Albert Sound. Bryan was relieved when Elias told them it was time to meet his mother.

"Come on, Bry and I will walk you there," Ellen offered.

"No, I'm going the opposite way. You guys don't want to miss your movie. See you later."

Bryan was silent as they made their way up the hill to the theatre. The pizza sat like a stone in his stomach.

"Which flick do you want to see?" he asked Ellen.

"How about the spooky one?" she said, pointing to a poster that showed a man with bear claws on his fingers and a face like melted plastic.

"Sure."

They bought their tickets and went inside, after Ellen had studied the poster for the other movie, a Disney about some animals. She wanted to be able to describe it to her parents when she got home. They didn't allow her to see horror movies, Bryan knew, because they believed stories with witches or ghosts in them were sacrilegious.

"Damn," Bryan said after he counted his change.

"What's the matter?"

"The woman short-changed me a buck."

"Let's go back."

"Never mind. I don't want to make an issue out of it. It doesn't matter."

"Sure it does," Ellen said. "Here, I'll do it." And she grabbed the change from his hand and went outside to the ticket booth. In a minute she returned and handed him the money.

"So what's bugging you today?" she said as they took their seats in the dark, almost deserted theatre.

"Nothing."

"You seem mad about something."

Bryan didn't answer. If he told her, he'd look stupid.

"Aren't you having fun?"

"You think I'm a wimp, don't you?" he blurted. "Because I wouldn't go back for my change."

"What? No, of course not."

"You and Elias seemed to be having a lot of fun," he said after a moment.

"What's wrong with that?" Ellen tried to read Bryan's face in the dark. "I like kidding around with him."

"I'm not, though."

"Not what?"

"Funny. Lots of laughs," said Bryan, knowing he was whining and angry at himself for it. "Why don't you go out with Elias if you like being with him so much?"

"I could. He's asked me enough times."

"*What?* He —"

"Shhhhhh. Not lately, Bryan. Take it easy, will you? Before you and I started going together."

They sat in silence. A corny Frank Sinatra tune leaked insipidly from the speakers overhead.

"So why didn't you?" Bryn asked.

"Because I didn't want to. Elias is nice and all, but he isn't really my type."

"Sure didn't seem like that today."

"Come on, Bry, you're not going to give me that jealous boyfriend routine, are you? The possessive male and all that revolting stuff? You don't need to feel that way. For one thing, I'm with you, right? For another, Elias is your best friend."

I thought he was, Bryan mused. "The movie's starting," he said as the lights dropped and Sinatra was cut off in mid-lament.

"Listen," Ellen whispered, drawing close. Her hair smelled clean and fresh. "You're my boyfriend. Now stop worrying." She leaned close and kissed him.

Bryan held her hand as he watched the movie.

Bryan and Ellen emerged from the theatre, blinking and squinting against the bright afternoon sun.

"Thank goodness," Ellen exclaimed. "The rain's gone."

Bryan sniffed. The odour of sulphur was almost physical. "So has the breeze. That stink is horrible. How can anyone live here?"

"You get used to it," Ellen said. "Sort of. In Nanaimo we smelled it a lot. But it was never this bad."

Just then they heard the clatter of the Wilsons' van and the beep of its horn. On the way back to Nootka Harbour, Ellen gave Elias and his mother a comic rendition of the horror movie, aided occasionally by Bryan, now in a much better mood. They laughed and joked all the way home. Even Mrs Wilson got in on the act, doing her Boris Karloff imitation, which was, Bryan thought, so bad it was extra-funny.

When they dropped Ellen off, she gave Bryan a big noisy kiss. He felt his face go as red as a strawberry. Elias smirked and Mrs Wilson pretended not to see.

When Bryan got home, his mother and Uncle Jimmy were sitting down to dinner. The radio on the counter blared country-western tunes, so Bryan knew his uncle had won the music war that day. Iris liked middle-of-the-road stuff. Bryan joined them as Jimmy dished out plates of steaming beef stew and thick slices of bread.

"You're just in time," Jimmy said, "for my famous Dead Cow Delight."

"Jimmy!" Iris complained. "We have to eat this glue, you know."

"And," Jimmy went on, unperturbed, "for an important announcement." He twisted caps off two bottles of beer and set them on the table. "So important, we have Kootenay champagne tonight."

"Wait," Iris interrupted. "Listen."

The six o'clock news had begun. *Premier Harrington announced today that licence has been granted for logging of the Orca Sound area of Vancouver Island, one of the last remaining untouched stands of temperate rainforest, not only in British Columbia but in the world. A spokesperson for Mackenzie Forest Industries said that the Orca Sound Ecological Preservation Plan, as the project is called, will create hundreds of jobs over the next five years —*

"Oh, my God!" Iris cried. "They can't !"

*The premier's announcement was immediately condemned by Greenpeace and other anti-logging groups, which warned that the decision will be fought in the courts. Action of a more direct nature was not ruled out.*

"Stupid buggers!" Jimmy threw down his fork

*Other logging projects in the past, at Tsitika, Walbran, Lyell Island, Carmanah and Stein were met with protests leading to the arrests of hundreds of people. Anti-logging activists warned that, if the clear-cut logging of Orca Sound proceeds, mass demonstrations and disruptions will be inevitable.*

*Clear-cut logging, long a controversial practice banned in most countries, was defended by —*

Jimmy jumped up and snapped off the radio. "Well, I guess my news isn't so good after all," he said bitterly.

"Those damn crooked politicians have caved in again!" Iris shouted. "All the corporations have to do is say 'jobs' and the politicians do whatever the company wants. Pardon? Sorry, Jimmy, I was ranting, wasn't I. What was it you wanted to tell us?"

Bryan's uncle said, "Well, I landed a job today."

"Great!" Bryan said.

"Terrific, Jimmy." Iris got up from the table and hugged her brother.

Jimmy struggled free. "You won't think it's so terrific when I tell you what it is."

Bryan saw the cloud pass over his mother's face. "You don't mean —"

"Yeah, I do mean. MFI is taking on about seventy-five people here and in Talbot Inlet."

"And you're one of them."

"I'm a logger, Iris. It's what I do."

"But, Jimmy." Iris fought to control herself. "I'm glad you found work, but . . . you can't."

His voice rising with every word, his face reddening, Jimmy said, "Why can't I? First hint of work I've had in a year or more. What am I supposed to do, turn it down and become a bloody tree-hugger?"

"They're going to clear-cut the Sound! Didn't you hear?" Iris responded, her own voice taking on a hard edge. "Do you want to look out over the passage and see raped mountainsides?"

"Don't be so damned dramatic, Iris. It won't be that bad and you know it. You always have to get hysterical and exaggerate. You know, I'm sick and tired of you people. I've been a logger all my life. Used to be I could be proud to say that, hold up my head. Now, for the last few years, me and guys like me are bad guys. Where the hell do you think the timber came from that this house is made out of? Eh, Iris? Where did the cedar grow that got cut down so you and that *other* committee you belong to could build the town's art gallery? From the forest around here, that's where! And people like me cut the timber down. We were good guys then, though, eh? Well, I'll tell you something, sister of mine, I'm *proud* to be a logger. And it's crazies like you that put me out of work to begin with!"

Bryan saw the familiar look of determination on his mother's face. "Jimmy, that forest has to be preserved."

Red-faced, Jimmy smashed his chair against the table, upsetting his untasted bottle of beer. Amber liquid cascaded to the floor. Bryan could see the jaw muscles flexing beneath Jimmy's skin. "And I need to work!" he shouted, slamming the kitchen door as he left the house.

Iris rushed to the door and grabbed the knob, but did not turn it. She faced Bryan. "I'd better get on the phone to the committee," she said quietly, almost to herself. "We've got to get organized, fast."

"Mom," Bryan said, "you were pretty hard on him."

She let out a long sigh. "This can't be allowed to happen."

"Why not? I mean, half the people around here work in the logging business, one way or the other," he said, thinking of Ellen's family as well as his own. "It's not like there aren't enough trees."

"That's just it. There aren't."

"Are you kidding? Jimmy's right, Mom. You're exaggerating. The whole island is a blanket of trees. Who's going to even notice? Besides, MFI replants the areas they log. We learned all about it in school."

"Listen, Bryan. In the first place, the sound is public land. Or, if you're First Nation, it's native land. Either way, it doesn't belong to MFI."

"Yeah, but they've got the tree farm licence, the rights to —"

"They buy those TFLs for a song because their goons in the legislature help them out. Then when they cut, they pay ridiculously low stumpage fees." Iris laughed bitterly. "And if the government changes its mind and cancels the TFLs, they have to pay the company millions of dollars in compensation. To get back the so-called rights to our own land! It's all as crooked as hell. Look, son," Iris said, calming down a little, "this isn't just another logging project. Everybody seems to think the rainforest is limitless. That's the way we treated the ozone layer, the air we breathe, the rivers and oceans. But those ancient stands of timber aren't limitless. When they're cut down, they're gone. All I'm saying is let's preserve what's left."

"But, Mom —"

"Take Vancouver Island," Iris interrupted. Bryan

knew that when she was on a roll like this, the best thing to do was stand back and let her wind down. "There are about ninety watersheds bigger than five thousand hectares, okay? You know how many of the ninety *haven't* been logged out?" Without waiting for his reply, she pounded her fist into her palm. "*Five!* There are five left, Bryan, and three of them are in Orca Sound! Some of the trees practically within sight of Nootka Harbour are a hundred metres high, way older than a thousand years. They can't be replaced. MFI wants to turn them into logs to sell to the States and Japan!"

When his mother paused for a breath and a pull on her beer, Bryan said, "But, Mom, the government makes sure that the forests are protected, doesn't it? I mean, look at the parks."

"The government is at the beck and call of the big corporations. The government allowed the streams to be polluted by mining and pulp companies. The government doesn't even follow its own laws. There are First Nation reserves right here on the island, which are under the control of the government, whose sewage systems don't meet government regulations! These are the officials you trust to protect the forests? The *people* have to protect the environment *from* the government!"

Putting down her beer, she repeated, "I've got to make some calls," and rushed into the family room.

Bryan sat at the kitchen table, staring at three plates of cold, untouched stew.

# SEVEN

M r Calder, whom his students called Nose Hairs because of the untrimmed sprouts that poked from his nostrils like reeds through the surface of a pond, told Bryan's Science class one day about Isaac Newton. That physicist, famous for allowing an apple to fall on his head and thus demonstrate the immutable law of gravity, had announced to the world that time always flows by at the same rate. On the other hand, lectured Nose Hairs, Einstein argued that time passes at differing rates, depending on a number of factors that Brian, numb with boredom, promptly forgot.

All in all, Bryan allowed that he had to side with Einstein, because he knew for a fact that when he was with Ellen, the hours flashed by. But in certain other places, like Talbot Inlet Junior High, time passed with the rapidity of a slug travelling uphill.

Norm's B&B provided excitement, but not the kind Bryan would go out of his way to find. Between his mother and his uncle, things were tense. Iris and Jimmy weren't trashing each other — their family love and loyalty was far too strong — but the line they had drawn between them was broad and clear. They conversed in toneless one-word sentences. They were silent at meals. For Bryan, living in his house was like walking barefoot through briars. So he spent a lot of his time at Ellen's and, when her parents set her to one of the many jobs they always seemed to find for her, he went to see Elias, whose parents left him pretty much alone. Bryan also helped Walter out on a few more whale-watching trips and, when the migrations had passed by, Walter hinted around a few times and Bryan helped him crabbing. Walter was not one to fall into a routine, so Bryan concluded that here again Einstein's theory of time won out.

Bryan's mother was driving herself frantic, working crazy hours at the supermarket — what her boss called open shifts, which allowed him to classify her as part-time and therefore not entitled to benefits — and agitating against the government's Orca Sound Ecological Preservation Plan. On street corners and outside the liquor store she could be found, in her sloppy pink track suit and green raincoat, handing out pamphlets. When she was at home she usually had the phone clamped between shoulder and jaw as she talked and made notes. It did not surprise Bryan that she was voted unanimously to be the chair of the SOS (Save Orca Sound) Committee. She went out and bought a fax machine, along with a dozen bundles of recycled paper, and it wasn't long before the committee was in contact with

Greenpeace and other sympathizers all over B.C., the rest of Canada, the States and Europe.

Under normal circumstances Bryan might have been proud of her. But he had to admit to himself that he resented the unwelcome changes in his daily routine and the strained relationship among the three of them. He was irritated by the artificial silence of his home and embarrassed by Iris's activism in the community. Around Jimmy he felt guilty because his mother was, in a sense, trying to take his uncle's job away. Around his mother he felt culpable because he got on so well with Jimmy the tree-raper — and because, deep down, he thought his mother was going too far.

The logging was scheduled to begin in June. Meanwhile, Jimmy worked on a crew pushing roads into the Big Bear and Salmon peninsulas so the heavy equipment and lumber trucks could get to the stands of old-growth forest that MFI wanted to cut down. In the late spring, Greenpeace and some other groups challenged the logging decision in court, but they lost. Iris said that she was not at all surprised: MFI owned the courts as well as far too many politicians. Jimmy countered with the opinion that she was paranoid, that soon she'd claim there were MFI agents in the mailbox and under her bed.

Bryan tried to ignore the increasing tension at home and in the community as he began a new experience. With Ellen's help he actually studied for exams. And he discovered, when reading the stack of whale books Ellen had lent him, that when he was interested in a topic, the facts and theories connected with it stuck in his mind like burrs on wool, and when he talked about these theories and facts, he actually felt smart. But information in school books had an irritating habit of staying in the books: only seldom did it take up residence in Bryan's memory.

And so the Einstein spring dragged on into June, and the first summer tourists trickled onto Vancouver Island. Strange camper-vans and RVs appeared on the streets; the restaurants bustled; the supermarket's aisles seemed perpetually jammed. Elias got a part-time job at Pacific Sands Provincial Park, just down the highway between Nootka Harbour and Talbot Inlet, filling out camping permits and doing light maintenance — a job Bryan would have loved, but he was the chief housekeeper and breakfast cooker at Norm's B&B.

Bryan, Ellen and Elias celebrated the last day of school by going out for burgers and making a nuisance of themselves in the restaurant — Elias like to chew his ice cubes, slurp his cola and perform other feats that threw Ellen into hysterics. Bryan, feeling the icy stares of the diners around them, figured that Ellen's high-pitched giggles were the most irritating of all the unwelcome sounds emanating from their table. After the meal, the three friends went over to Elias's house for a video binge: three horror movies in a row, all chosen by Ellen.

"What a rebel you are," Elias told her.

While Bryan, his mother and uncle were having one of their silent suppers the next day, the phone rang. Bryan heard the switcher transfer the call to the fax machine in the family room. Iris rose and went to her little SOS command post by the bay window that looked out over Osprey Cove. Bryan and his uncle continued to attack their bowls of spaghetti. Iris returned to the table, a piece of flimsy paper in her hand and a happy look on her face.

"It's all set. We're going to blockade the bridge across the Big Bear River starting July first, Canada Day." She sat down and twirled spaghetti around her fork. "I'm going to be there," she said, "on the line."

A deep silence followed. Bryan's forkful of spaghetti remained halfway to his mouth. He looked at his mother, then at his uncle, not surprised to see Jimmy's face flush and his jaw muscles flexing. Jimmy quietly laid his fork and spoon across his dish.

"Well, Iris, I guess I'll see you there. Only, I'll be on the other side."

Bryan sat between them, immobilized by their determined stares, trapped in their silence.

# PART TWO:

# Summer

# ONE

Painting a fence was not Bryan's idea of a patriotic act, but Canada Day found him on his knees at the edge of the driveway, resentfully slapping his brush against the first of 179 pickets that stretched away to the mailbox at the roadside. He had put off the job for weeks, and today Iris had put her foot down.

"It's been dry and sunny for two days," she had pointed out. "So today you get the job done before it rains again."

First he had had to scrape the loose and flaking paint from the fence, a messy and cosmically boring job, not quite as tedious or messy as the actual painting, which he had just begun when the batteries on his portable radio had died.

"Damn!" he said, whacking the picket before him with a full brush that sent a spiteful shower of white paint splashing across his face. He jammed the brush into the paint can and wiped his cheek with a rag, smearing the greasy liquid all over his face.

"Damn!"

"Hey, son. Is this Norm's B&B?"

Bryan turned, rag in hand, to the van at the end of the drive. There were two men in the cab. He nodded, getting to his feet.

The stranger drove up the driveway and parked at the house. Ontario plates, Bryan noted, watching the men step onto the porch at the kitchen door, knock and enter. These must be the tree-huggers Mom told me about — the ones who contacted her through Greenpeace, looking for a place to stay, close to the action. More work for me, making beds, vacuuming, doing laundry. Oh, well, we can sure use the money. He went back to his Canada Day job.

A few minutes later the men came out of the house and started unpacking the van. "Got a second to help us out?" one of them called.

He was a friendly-looking, muscular guy. His companion was tall and dark.

"You must be Bryan," he said, shaking hands. "Iris told us about you. I'm Kevin Campbell, and this is Otto."

"Hi," Bryan said.

"Nice to see you," Otto said, then slung a pack on his back and picked up a large rucksack.

"I'll show you the way," Bryan offered. "The door to the basement is around the other side. You have your own entrance."

"Nice," Kevin commented after Bryan had shown them the two rooms. "This will be great."

"You're from Ontario, eh?" Bryan asked.

"Yep. Drove all the way from Toronto. We wanted to come out and do our bit. You know, protest the logging. We're glad to hear your mom is on the right side. We think it's a crime, what they're doing to the forests. Right, Otto?"

"Damn right. Shouldn't be allowed."

The last thing Bryan wanted was a conversation about trees, so he left his mother's new supporters and got back to work on the fence. He had coated about a dozen more pickets when Iris came out of the house and stood with her hands on her hips, surveying the job.

Far too cheerily for Bryan's mood she said, "Good work, Rembrandt. It has a sort of quiet intensity, a sort of—"

"Bye, Mom. Have fun at the supermarket."

Iris laughed and walked on down the drive, waving as she turned onto the road leading into town.

Not long after, Bryan's labours were disturbed again.

"Reminds me of Tom Sawyer."

Bryan looked up at Kevin, squinting against the sun high in the sky. "Yeah, I guess."

"Looks like you could use a little help."

"No, it's okay. Thanks anyway."

"Come on, where do you keep your paintbrushes? I feel like a little activity after all the driving me and Otto have been doing."

Bryan found another paintbrush and Kevin started at the far end of the fence. For an hour they slowly worked toward one another.

"Your mom says you're the chief cook and bottle-washer around here," Kevin said when he had reached Bryan's side.

"Yeah, that's me." Bryan smiled, happy to be almost finished the job and grateful to their new guest.

"You do the laundry, clean up the rooms, cook."

"Yeah."

"Tell you what. Otto and me, we're not too fussy about starched sheets and dusted furniture, two bachelors like us. We both like our privacy. So let's say we just forget about you cleaning up our rooms. And as for washing the sheets and pillowcases, we'll just leave the linen in the hall outside our rooms once a week."

"Well . . ."

"You'd be doing us a big favour." Kevin smiled. "And naturally we'd keep it a secret between you and us. Okay?"

"If that's what you want."

The big man winked and patted Bryan on the shoulder. "Good man, Bryan." He handed Bryan the paintbrush.

"Thanks for your help, Kevin."

"No sweat."

If Bryan had been slightly anxious that his mother would discover and disapprove of his arrangement with Kevin, his worries evaporated over the next few days. He hardly saw her. Instead, he would find notes on the kitchen table: *I'll be at work until five* or *I've got an SOS meeting 'til late. Your supper's in the oven or I'll be at the peace camp all morning. I'll go to work from there. See you tonight.*

The peace camp was the name the activists gave to their rallying point out by the Big Bear River bridge. What a laugh, Bryan thought. I don't feel any peace.

The anti-logging protests began early in July, just as Iris had predicted. The tree-huggers, as Jimmy called them, blocked the bridge when the lumber trucks, laden with fresh-cut timber, tried to cross the Big Bear River. A few days later MFI obtained, in what Iris bitterly termed "record time," a court injunction that forbade blockage of the road or bridge. The court order did not exactly strike fear into the hearts of the protesters, she said. On the day that the injunction came into effect, fifty-five people were arrested.

When Bryan dragged himself out of bed the next morning, later than usual, the house was quiet except for the hum of rain on the roof. He padded down the hall in his bare feet and found another of his mother's notes. Knowing what it would say, he tossed it aside. He slipped down to the basement and listened for a moment. Kevin and Otto had left, probably to the peace camp.

Alone in the house, feeling like the only sane person in the universe, he put the coffee on and phoned Ellen. They talked for an hour or so. She was not allowed out that day, she said. "It's clean-the-basement day."

He was tearing into a plate of bacon, eggs and toast, reading a book on humpback whales, when the phone rang. Probably Elias, Bryan thought. His friend had the day off, and the two of them planned to go down to the tiny arcade near the government dock and play a few video games. If the place wasn't crawling with tourists' kids bored from the rain in the campsites.

The male voice was businesslike. "Is this Norm's B&B?"

"Yes, it is. But we're full up for the next — "

"Does Jimmy Lormer live there?"

"Yes."

"This is Scott Weatherby. His foreman at MFI."

"He's at work today. He left —"

"Jimmy's had an accident."

Time stopped for Bryan. He was standing beside his mother in their living room above the store in Drumheller. Her knuckles whitened as she clutched the telephone. Her face was pale. She asked, "Are you sure it's him? Are you certain it's Norm?" and then she sobbed, "No, no, no, no . . ." as Bryan was gripped tighter and tighter by a terror he had never imagined.

The voice snatched him back. "Are you there?"

"Is it bad?" he asked. He held his breath.

"Pretty bad. You'd —"

"Is he alive?"

"He's alive, yeah. But he's pretty smashed up, looks like. We're taking him to the hospital now. You better get his sister."

Bryan slammed down the phone and dashed next door. He pounded on the door, praying that Walter was home.

# TWO

Walter's ancient pick-up truck rattled down Highway 93, its bald tires hissing on the pavement, its wipers flapping ineffectually across the cracked windshield. Walter sat grim-faced at the wheel, peering ahead into the rain. Beside him on the torn seat, Bryan willed the truck to go faster.

He was flung against the door when Walter swerved off 93, throwing the truck into a slide when it hit the gravel bush road. The thick conifers closed in around them. After a few moments jouncing along the narrow road, the truck broke out of the forest into an extensive and barren moonscape. The slopes on both sides of the road had been clear-cut and burned years before. Blackened stumps poked out of the denuded ground. Bryan remembered that Iris and her committee had dubbed this huge clear-cut "The Wasteland." Large signs had been painted on plywood and nailed to posts held upright by piles of rocks: *Orca Sound, Not Clear-Cut Sound* and *Vancouver Island, Brazil of the North*.

Walter steered the truck around a bend and suddenly the peace camp loomed ahead in the drizzle. Dozens of tents had been pitched in the flatter areas of the Wasteland, making blue, orange and red blotches in a landscape of muted greys and greens. Hundreds of men, women and children in ponchos or raincoats milled around.

Walter brought the pick-up to a shuddering halt next to a huge tent with a poster, *Rainforest Café*, nailed to a stump beside the door. "Maybe she's in there, your mother," he said, uttering his first words since Bryan had banged on the screen door of his trailer.

Bryan led the way into the tent. A few dozen people were seated at tables, spooning soup out of bowls, cups and tins. Behind a trestle table a woman in a food-stained apron served soup out of a cauldron to a line-up of wet activists. Bryan asked her if his mother was around. The woman knew Iris but had not seen her that day. Bryan explained why he was looking for her.

"Oh, God. Just a minute." The woman threw down the ladle and hustled to the corner of the tent, where a man sat at a card table. Before him, a laptop computer, two portable FM radios and several cellular telephones were neatly arranged. The woman spoke to him briefly, then returned to tell Bryan that Iris was up the road at the bridge.

Bryan and Walter jumped back into the truck. The road narrowed, dirt replacing the gravel. This must be the new section Jimmy helped build, Bryan thought with a deepening sense of foreboding. Naked stumps lined the track where trees had been felled, and piles of forest debris marked the work of the bulldozers.

The road dipped and the truck rattled into an open area jammed with a chaotic array of people and vehicles, as if some madman had decided to set up a carnival in the middle of the forest. A yellow school bus, three RCMP cruisers and a police van with wire mesh on the windows were parked on both sides of the road. Walter parked behind the police van.

Just ahead, a knot of protesters stood listening to a woman speaking through a megaphone.

"Who is willing to be arrested?" Bryan heard as he approached.

A few hands went up. A girl of about ten — Bryan had seen her around town — put up her hand. "I'll have to ask my mother first," she yelled, pushing damp bangs away from her eyes. No one laughed.

"All right," the woman continued, her voice metallic and impersonal as it squeezed through the megaphone. "Remember, when you join the people on the bridge, that we are totally committed to non-violence. When the process server reads the injunction, be silent: the judge will treat you more harshly if you do not show respect when the injunction is read. Do not resist the police. Let your body go limp and allow them to carry you to the bus. Don't even hold on to them as they carry you away: if you do, they'll charge you with resisting arrest. Good luck, and save Orca Sound!"

The crowd around her took up the chant as they moved slowly toward the bridge. Bryan darted among them as quickly as he could, anxiously searching for his mother. At the edge of the throng, just up the rise at the side of the road, he caught sight of Otto and Kevin, taking pictures. They look like reporters covering a car wreck, Bryan thought.

Bryan caught up to the woman with the megaphone. Shouting above the chanting, he asked her if Iris was nearby.

"Yeah, she's around here someplace." Before Bryan could explain, the woman vanished into the crowd.

Bryan had no choice but to follow them. The road fell away more steeply as it descended to the river. He could see the bridge now, with the Big Bear River foaming beneath it on its way to Gray's Passage. On the bridge about a dozen people were sitting quietly in the drizzle, several rows deep, facing in Bryan's direction. The road rising uphill on the other side was empty.

"See her yet?" Walter had materialized out of the crowd.

Bryan shook his head and began to jog downhill. A car pushed along behind him, horn blaring, forcing him to the side of the road. It was the first of a convoy. Elias's brother, Zeke, who had joined the RCMP about a year before, was in one of the cruisers.

As the last car passed him, Bryan saw a flash of pink up on the bridge. A shade of pink all too familiar to him. He peered through the drizzle. Two pink knees stuck out from under a dark green poncho. It was Iris, sitting cross-legged in the second row.

Like a lit match, anger flared through him. He began to run. You idiot, he thought. Your brother is on his way to the hospital and you're out here with a bunch of crazies sitting on a bridge and getting your ass wet. "Who is willing to be arrested?" the megaphone woman had asked. As if they were at a carnival and this was all a big game.

"Mom!" Bryan shouted, jumping up and down, waving.

Things began to happen quickly. The cars stopped at the river's edge. Doors flew open and cops walked toward the bridge, accompanied by a bald man in a trench coat. On the other side of the bridge, a lumber truck appeared at the top of the hill, laden with four mammoth trees, and on each side of the truck was a column of people, walking silently.

There were men, women and children in the columns. Each of them waved a yellow ribbon. Most wore yellow or red hardhats. A few signs bobbed up and down: *We Want to Work* and *Obey the Law*.

As the truck and its silent escort slowly approached the bridge, the bald man raised a megaphone. He sounded impersonal, even a little bored. He told the protesters that they were in violation of a court injunction that forbade such actions. "If you are not off the bridge before that truck stops moving, you will be put under arrest." The megaphone dropped out of sight. The man walked back to his car as if he didn't care whether the people had heard him or not.

Bryan's fear grew with every metre covered by the big yellow logging truck. The crowd around him took up the chant again: "Save Orca Sound!" And now the counter-protest gave voice: "Let us work!"

The truck was on the bridge now, inching toward Bryan's mother, its diesel engine barely audible above the chanting war. Cops marched purposefully onto the bridge. The truck came on, its huge grille towering over the silent, seated protesters.

"Mom! Mom! I have to talk to you! Dammit, get out of there!" Bryan screamed, pushing toward the bridge.

It was no use. The eighteen-wheeler came to a halt inches from the backs of the protesters. The counterpro-testers formed a wall, waving their ribbons and rhythmi-cally demanding to be allowed to work. Shoving two or three people out of the way, Bryan stepped onto the bridge.

"Mom! Uncle Jimmy —"

A burly cop pushed him back. "Take one more step on this bridge and I'll have to arrest you. Now get away."

"But I have to —"

The cop pushed again. Bryan fell backward. He scrambled to his feet, looking around frantically for Walter. The police were carrying protesters away and dumping them in the back of the blue van.

And then Bryan saw Zeke Wilson and another cop lugging his mother, like a drenched pink bag of sand, off the bridge.

# THREE

Brian stood helplessly at the side of the road, watching the strange convoy. Two police cruisers drove slowly up the hill, their revolving lights flickering through the fog to the green wall of forest. Behind them, the yellow school bus with a few faces showing in the windows, then the van full of prisoners. And last, the huge eighteen-wheeler snorting along, hauling four trees out of the bush, flanked by people waving yellow ribbons.

When the truck had ground past him, Bryan saw Walter standing at the side of the road. His arms were crossed and, to Bryan's surprise, he looked angry. He looked, in fact, as though he'd been saving up a few decades' worth of anger and now it was forcing its way out. When Bryan reached him he turned and began to walk to his truck.

Bryan tramped along, head down in the rain, furtively searching for faces he knew — so he could avoid them. He did not want to be recognized, not where his mother had been picked up — literally, he thought without humour — for making fools of her whole family.

He climbed into Walter's truck and they moved off, creeping along the road crowded with activists. She should be at her brother's side, he thought, not playing politics out here in the bush. Rain beat on the roof of the truck, the wipers flapped, streaking the windshield, the old motor strained and grumbled, pushing the truck past the café and through the Wasteland. Not since his dad had been killed had Bryan felt so depressed and empty. His mother was on her way to jail, his uncle on his way to hospital.

Walter drove straight to Nootka Harbour's small hospital and pulled up at the Emergency entrance. Bryan jumped down and ran through the automatic doors. He skidded to a halt in front of the desk and told the old woman behind the glass that he was Jimmy Lormer's nephew. After clicking a few computer keys, she told Bryan that a doctor would be with him soon.

He sat down in a plastic armchair just as Walter entered the waiting room. Bryan wondered if he looked as wet and bedraggled as Walter did. Across the room a young mother waited, a toddler with a runny nose squirming in her lap. Bryan fidgeted. He drummed his fingers on the chair arms. He crossed and recrossed his ankles. He flipped through a four-month-old magazine and tossed it back onto the coffee table.

Jimmy must be pretty bad, he thought, or they would have said something to me right away. If he was okay, the

lady at reception would have said so. I wonder if —
Bryan did not want to complete the thought. He felt an
ache in his throat and suddenly his eyes filled with tears.
He wiped them away quickly, stealing a glance at the
woman nearby.

Mom should be here, he thought. She's so damn self-
ish with her stupid causes. She —

"Bryan Troupe?"

Bryan jumped from his seat, eyes riveted on the doctor who stood in the doorway of the waiting room, holding a clipboard. His heart raced. Here it comes.

"Would you come with me, please."

Walter and Bryan followed her into a small consulting room. She pushed the door shut behind them.

"Is he . . . ?" Bryan asked.

"He's not in danger." The doctor reported that she
had set Jimmy's arm, which had been broken badly in
two places, upper and lower. His leg was sprained and
bruised. She had also treated his abrasions and contu-
sions. "That's cuts and bruises," she added. "He's in
recovery and he's sedated."

"That's it?"

"That's it, yes. If you want to call a mangled arm and
a general mauling 'it'."

"He's okay!" Bryan exclaimed to Walter, who nodded. Then, to the doctor, "Can we see him?"

"Not for a few hours, I'm afraid. By then, visiting
hours will be over, so you might as well go home and
come back tomorrow."

Dog gave them a howling welcome, dancing on the end of his leash.

"How about I make us a pot of coffee, Walter, after we get into some dry clothes?" Bryan said as they pulled into the driveway and parked by the trailer.

Walter nodded and entered his trailer.

Bryan's limbs felt heavy and lazy as he took a hot shower, then dressed in jeans and his warmest shirt to drive away the chill that had settled in his bones.

He went down to the kitchen and called Ellen's number. When no one answered he looked up the number for the police station. Before the ringing started on the other end, he slammed down the phone. "The hell with her," he hissed.

Walter pushed open the door, removed his boots and took a chair. Bryan poured the coffee, set out milk and sugar.

Walter took a noisy sip. "Interesting day."

"That's for sure. I'm glad Jimmy's okay."

"He's a pretty tough guy, your uncle."

Bryan realized, as he studied the weathered face across from him, that Walter must have been worried, too. He was fond of Jimmy — of all Bryan's family, for that matter.

"Your mom's pretty tough, too," Walter added.

Yeah, that's one word to describe her, Bryan thought. Stupid is another. Bryan reminded himself that when you were with Walter you had to listen carefully to his silences. Was Walter trying to tell him not to worry about his mom? Well, he wasn't worried about her at all. She'd be okay. It was Bryan who would have to go out tomorrow and wonder if everybody would stare at him or point to him behind his back and gossip. That's Iris Troupe's kid. She's in jail, you know. She got hauled away like a load of wood by the cops. You'd think a woman would have more pride. And that pink track suit. I tell you!

"Some people don't appreciate what she's trying to do," Walter said.

"You think she should have been out there in the rain getting a police record?" Bryan shot back. "Making a fool of herself?"

The kitchen was silent. With a sigh, Walter got up and replenished the two mugs. He sat down again and stirred his coffee slowly.

"Long time ago," he began in a low, almost expressionless voice, "this whole area used to be my peoples.' Well, us Nootkas lost the land and we're all scattered now. Some of us still believe the spirits of our ancestors don't go away to some kind of afterlife like the Christians talk about. Me, I think the ghosts of the dead stay near the living. My ancestors' spirits are walking over there on Big Bear and Salmon, Flower Pot Island, Vickers Island. We got different names for those places in our language. The spirits are still walking in the old forests, along the creekbeds and the beaches."

Walter blew on his coffee and took a drink. Bryan waited.

"Now the tree-cutters are gonna drive them away from their ancient lands for good. I worry sometimes, wondering where they can go."

Bryan thought for a moment before he said, "Do you think the spirits will leave if only a few trees — you know, the real big ones — are harvested?"

Walter smiled. "Interesting word, that. 'Harvested.' Like them guys are ploughing up potatoes, knowing next year they can come back and there'll be a new crop ready for them to take. An ancient rainforest isn't a field of wheat. You don't 'harvest' a thousand-year-old tree. If you cut it down, you cancel it for good."

"Yeah, I see what you mean," Bryan admitted, wondering once again what there was about the way Walter talked that made things so clear.

"I hope you won't take no offence, Bryan," Walter said gently, "but maybe you don't know what I mean. Some people think they can go into a forest, take the trees they want, leave the slash and bark and the timber that don't pay lying around, and nothing changes. They think the forest is just like it was before they came. Only a few trees are missing. They don't know. The whole thing — sea, sky, forest — it's all connected."

Walter joined his thumbs and index fingers to form a circle. "They're all one. Change part of it, it's all changed. We know that, us first peoples. That's why, in all our bands, all our nations, the circle is a main symbol."

Walter held up his mug, took a sip, looked at

Bryan over the rim.

"You remember the time last spring when you fell out of the boat?"

Bryan laughed softly. "I sure do."

"You heard the whales." It was not a question.

How did he know? Bryan thought. Ellen was the only person he had told. "Yeah, I heard them."

"I hope you won't take offence, my friend. You heard them singing, but you don't know yet what they were telling you."

"You . . . This is weird. You think they were *talking* to me?"

"I think everything in nature — bear, eagle, raven, even trees — they all talk to us. The earth speaks, but nowadays not too many of us listen any more. Far as I can tell, whites have never listened."

Before Bryan could answer, the phone rang.

"Bryan? Zeke Wilson. I'm calling from the station. Listen, Bryan, I feel really bad about what happened today. With your mom and all. I . . . I just wanted to call and tell you they're processing Iris right now, and she'll be released in about an hour."

"Okay, Zeke."

"And, Bryan, I won't get a chance to talk to her. Will you tell her how sorry I am?"

"Sure, Zeke. I'll let her know."

Bryan hung up, then told Walter what Zeke had said.

"He's okay, Zeke is. For a cop." Walter stood and drained his cup. "We'll go pick her up."

"I'm not going," Bryan said. "I'll wait here."

Bryan felt pinned by Walter's gaze. "Okay, then."

"Walter, can I ask you something?"

"Don't see why not."

"Well, considering the way you feel — you know, the stuff we were just talking about — how come you're not in the movement with Mom?"

"Well, between you and me, I guess I had a couple of brushes with the cops a few years ago. I learned to steer clear of cops as much as I can."

As he went out the door he added, "Maybe you got something there, though."

# FOUR

Iris asked about her brother as soon as she entered the house, and Bryan told her what he knew.

"Thank God he'll be able to use his arm again," she said, hanging up her poncho and shrugging out of her sweater. "Walter told me Jimmy was all right but — you know Walter — no details. I had nightmares all the way home that Jimmy had lost the arm. I've seen that happen in some of those logging accidents." Bryan's mother raked her fingers through her damp hair. "Well, I'm going to have a bath and get to bed. I have to be at the supermarket at eight tomorrow."

"You want some hot tea or something, Mom?"

"No, thanks, dear. Just my nice comfortable bed. It's been a long day. What were you up to?"

Bryan knew then that Walter hadn't told his mother that they had been out to the river. She didn't know Bryan had seen her picked up and thrown into the police van.

"Well," he began, "as a matter of fact, Mom —" and he quit when he saw the tiredness and stress in her face.

"Umm," he began again, "I just, you know, got my work done at home and hung around."

"That's nice," she said. And she dragged herself down the hall to her bedroom.

The next morning, Bryan woke early to the smell of toast and the scrape of a kitchen chair — his mother was having breakfast. Sitting up, he stuffed his pillow behind him, and leaned back against the wall and thought about what Walter had said the day before.

Although he respected his neighbour and had a lot of affection for him, Bryan could not buy all that talk about ghosts and spirits. A forest is a forest, he thought, not a spirit-land or a museum. It's pretty, sure, but a tree is a tree.

When he heard his mother leave, he got up, showered, dressed and began to prepare breakfast for the two guests. Kevin and Otto entered the kitchen all set for another day on the picket line, Bryan observed, dressed like real live outdoorsmen in their designer active wear, carrying backpacks with Greenpeace logos on them.

"So how's your mother?" Kevin asked, pouring syrup on a stack of pancakes.

Bryan stood with his back to the two men, ladling batter onto the frying pan. "She's fine, thanks."

"Glad to hear it. We really admire her commitment, right, Otto?"

"Not too many like her around," Otto said.

"And we're glad to be staying with kindred souls, so

to speak," Kevin continued. "Know what I mean, Tom?"

"Tom?" Bryan flipped the half dozen pancakes and turned to face the men.

Kevin smiled. "Remember the fence?"

Bryan laughed. "Yeah."

"So how about it? Are me and Otto in among kindred souls, like I said?"

"Well, not completely." Embarrassed, he turned to the stove again. "My uncle isn't exactly a tree-hugger."

"Really. That's too bad. Has a different view, does he?"

"Sort of."

"How about you, Tom?"

"I'm what you'd call neutral."

"Really. Well, I'm disappointed to hear that. Yes, sir. Oh, well."

"That Indian next door in the trailer," Otto said. "Is he in the movement?"

"He's Nootka," Bryan said. "He doesn't like to be called Indian."

"Whatever. Is he in the movement, then?"

Otto's voice seemed to push too hard for Bryan's liking. "I don't know," he said. "Anybody want more pancakes?"

"Not me," Kevin answered, gulping down the last of his coffee and pushing back his chair. "I'm done."

Otto rose, too, and began to pull on his jacket. Both men picked up their gear and went out the door.

That night Ellen came over for dinner, and when his mother got home — later than usual because she had dropped by the hospital to take some magazines and snacks to Jimmy — Bryan and Ellen had everything ready. Bryan used an original recipe of his uncle's, which involved egg noodles, some hamburger meat fried with onions and garlic, a dollop of tomato paste and grated cheese. Ellen expressed her scepticism all through the preparation but, when the dish came out of the oven, she pronounced it a success.

Iris slumped into her chair, exhausted. "I got no lunch and no breaks today," she said, "we were so busy. This is delicious. You two should open a restaurant."

"We'll call it the Clear-Cut Café," Bryan said. Ellen gave him a harsh look.

"Very funny, kid. Don't you start in on me. I've had a hard day and your uncle's already taken a few shots at me. I felt like breaking his other arm."

"I, for one, would like to hear about what went on yesterday, Mrs Troupe. Grumpy over there, with his mouth full, wouldn't tell me a thing." Bryan had asked Ellen not to tell his mother he had seen her arrested.

"Well, I can tell you that getting arrested isn't nearly as glamorous as it is on TV. When they dumped us — and 'dumped' is the right word for it; those cops weren't gentle — we were taken back to town and herded into a holding cell. About three dozen of us, I guess, including five or six kids and a few seniors. At the time we arrived the cops were still processing the fifty or so who had been arrested at dawn when they tried to block the trucks from going into the bush."

"You mean," Bryan cut in, "that your group was the *second* ?"

"Yup."

"It's disgusting," said Ellen.

"It sure is," Bryan chimed in.

"They ought to be ashamed of themselves," Ellen added. "Treating you people like that. As if you were criminals."

Bryan almost choked on his last mouthful of Noodles James.

"Go on, Mrs Troupe," Ellen urged.

"Well, there's not much more to tell. We were charged with contempt of court and asked to sign what the legal beagles call an undertaking that we would appear for our trials — where the hell are we going to go; almost all of us live around here — and that we would not take part in any more road-blocking. About ten people refused to sign, so they were taken into Nanaimo to the minimum-security prison there."

"Good," Bryan hissed. Had Ellen forgotten that her father was a big gun in MFI and that her mother got most of her legal business from the company?

"Contempt of court," Ellen commented. "Doesn't sound too serious."

Iris sighed, putting down her fork and pushing her empty plate aside. "Actually, it is. Judges get very touchy when they feel the court's authority is flouted.

Sometimes I think a few of those buggers are a bit too vain about their powers. You can get quite a long sentence for contempt."

Bryan suddenly felt afraid. "Anyway, it's all over now for you, right, Mom? You signed, right? Or you wouldn't be here. They wouldn't have let you go."

"Yes and no."

Bryan groaned. Before he could ask what her enigmatic answer had meant, there was a loud knock on the door.

"I'll get it," Ellen said, rising. "I'm closest."

She pulled open the door, and in stepped two RCMP offcers. Imposing in their blue uniforms, the two men seemed to fill the small kitchen.

"Iris, we need to talk to you," one said. Bryan recognized him, but didn't know his name.

Without moving from her chair, Iris said, "Me? What's it about?"

"There's been an act of sabotage in the MFI equipment yard," the second cop announced dramatically. "A truck was fire-bombed."

"'Sabotage'?" Iris smirked. "What is this, a spy movie?"

"What's this got to do with Mrs Troupe?" Ellen demanded.

The cops ignored her. "This is Norm's Bed 'n Breakfast, isn't it?" the first cop said, hitching up his leather belt.

"You know it is, Nick, for God's sake," Iris said. "You

live in this town. I see you and your wife in the super-market once a week. What the hell does all this have to do with me?"

"You don't seem too upset about the sabotage," the second cop said. He was a lanky man with a bad sunburn.

"Why should I be?"

Wrong move, Mom, Bryan thought. He was aware that Ellen had come to Iris's defence but he had not, yet he could not think what to say or do.

Sunburn looked at Nick, who told Iris, "One of your business cards was found near the burned-out truck. You better come with us."

Iris seemed to lose all her energy at once. "Look, I've been through enough," she said.

At last Bryan found his voice. "You can't arrest her. She couldn't have done it. She's been at work all day and she's been here since she got off."

"We're not arresting you, Iris," Nick said. "But we'd like you to come down to the detachment and answer a few questions."

"Wait a minute!" Ellen shouted. "This —"

"You can make this easy, or you can make it hard," Sunburn snarled, earning a withering glance from his fellow officer.

"Let's make this simple for everybody concerned, eh?" Nick said quietly.

Iris pulled on her sweater and left the house between the two big men. Bryan stood in the kitchen, his heart beating quickly, his fists opening and closing.

Ellen began to clear the table. "Come on Bry, let's do the dishes."

Bryan moved as though his limbs were lead. This was worse than watching her get picked up out at the river, he thought. He had been mad at her then. She had been far away and he had watched everything unfold from the outside. It was different when two threatening men with guns came right into your home and took someone away. Not someone. His own mother. He felt violated, invaded. And if he felt this way, what must be going through his mother's mind?

"Ellen," he said, "could you stay for a while?"

Catching him by surprise as he picked up a plate and began to dry it, she kissed him. "Sure, I'll stay as long as you want."

They worked in silence, then Ellen cut in on his thoughts. "Are you still mad at her?"

"Wouldn't you be?" he asked, not meaning it.

"I don't know. All I've ever heard is MFI's side of things. Dad and Mom — who aren't exactly objective — say that the industry has changed its practices, that the clear-cuts are smaller now, and they try to be careful so there won't be big mud slides off the clear-cuts like there used to be. Then they replant the areas. And let's face it, the forestry is by far the biggest employer around here. Over in Talbot Inlet almost everybody is a logger. If the industry shut down, all those people would lose their livelihood, and Talbot Inlet would be a ghost town."

"Try and tell Mom and the tree-huggers that," Bryan

said, wishing that, when he argued with his mother, he could line up facts the way Ellen could.

"But the thing is," Ellen went on as she drained the sink and ran the dishrag over the countertop, "I really admire your mother."

"You do?"

"It takes a lot of guts to do what she's doing."

"Guts? Or . . . I don't know, stupid pills or something."

"That's not fair, Bry. She's just doing what she thinks is right."

Isn't *anybody* on my side? Bryan thought. The telephone rang.

It was Ellen's father, and he didn't sound too happy. Bryan handed her the phone. She listened for a minute, her forehead creased in a frown, and said "But —" and "Dad, that's not —" and "Okay. I said okay!"

"I have to go home," she said as she hung up.

"I figured."

Alone in the house again, Bryan tried to watch a sitcom, but he couldn't follow the story line and none of the jokes were funny. He went to his room, clapped his earphones on and turned up the volume on the stereo. Steel Needle's lyrics and heavy rock failed to calm him. He went back to the TV.

About an hour later, he heard his mother come in. He pushed the Mute button on the remote when she dropped into her favourite easychair and heaved a big sigh. Her hair was wet from the rain and there were dark circles under her eyes.

"I'd love a nice cold beer."

Bryan brought her a can of beer and a glass. Ignoring the tumbler, Iris took a long drink. Bryan watched the silent figures move across the screen.

"They had to let me go," his mother said finally. "Called Parker, my boss, at his house and asked if I'd been working at the supermarket all day. Then they grilled me. Who would have my business card? Did I know anybody who might burn up a truck? I told them we're non-violent. None of us believes in that action-movie crap. We're for passive resistance. We don't even bad-mouth the cops when they arrest us, let alone destroy property or try to hurt people.

"Then, as I was leaving, Zeke came up to me. Outside the station he told me that the truck that was burned was a worthless relic that's been up on blocks for over a year. He says the cops figured the fire was symbolic. That's why they suspected our committee." She laughed bitterly. "MFI is destroying one of the last stands of primal rainforest in the world and they're worried about a useless old truck!"

Iris drained her beer. "So, are you glad your mom's not an eco-terrorist?" She tried to laugh.

Bryan continued to stare at the screen.

"What's the matter, son?"

Bryan felt a tear form itself in the corner of his eye. "Everything's changed, Mom. Everything's gone bad."

"What do you mean? I thought you were doing fine lately. You got better marks in school than ever. You have a girlfriend. Or is it Jimmy?"

"It seems like everybody's mad at each other all the time, Mom. You and Jimmy. Me and you. The kids at school. The week before we got out for the summer, there were three fights. All because our parents were lined up on one side or the other on this stupid logging thing. It's no fun any more, living around here. Everybody's upset all the time."

"You want me to quit, don't you?" Iris said quietly.

"Why does it have to be you, Mom? And why can't people accept things? We can't do anything about MFI, even if we want to. And I don't. Neither does Jimmy."

Iris leaned back in her chair. The light from the lamp beside her crossed her face, showing the lines of fatigue. "I guess you're against me, too," she whispered. "I've been so busy, I never really noticed."

"I'm not against you, Mom. I just wish —"

"That I'd stop."

"I want things to be the way they used to be," he almost shouted.

Iris looked at her husband's picture on the mantel. "So do I," she said. "Son, life isn't like that. It isn't about getting what you want."

Bryan used the remote to turn off the silent television. He followed her line of sight to the photo of his father and felt a stab of grief, and a stronger stab of pity for his mother.

"Mom," he began hopefully, "don't you think you've been through enough? You've done your bit for the movement or whatever you call it. You got arrested. You got hassled. Nobody can say you haven't done your part. Now you can let it go and . . ."

"And what, son?"

"And . . . and we can go back to the way things were. Jimmy will be home soon."

"I can't."

"Why the hell not?" he shouted, suddenly angry again.

"Don't take that tone with me. I'm not in the mood."

"You're not in the mood? Well, I'm not in the mood to have my life screwed up because my mother is acting like a jerk!"

Iris's face turned red. "Look, Bryan Norman Troupe, there's more involved here than your life. Try and look beyond yourself a little."

"I'm sorry, Mom." He tried to marshal his thoughts. "It's just that . . . ah, the hell with it."

Iris rose from her chair and padded into the kitchen. She returned with a fresh can of beer. She poured it slowly into her glass.

"Remember how your dad used to brag about how smooth he could pour beer?"

"Yeah. He could get one finger-breadth of foam every time."

"I want to explain this to you," she began. "To try to make you understand. Okay?"

You'll never be able to do that, Bryan thought. But he said, "Yeah."

"It's complicated, but it's simple, too. I mean, the issues and the situations and the propaganda can be confusing, and if you're not careful, you can get so damn mixed up you lose your way and don't know what to do. But when I was a little girl my gram gave me an old beat-up book to read. I can't even remember the title — isn't that strange? — but I can recall everything else about it. The green cover that was worn through to the cardboard at the corners. The split in the spine. The pages curled up on the edges because they'd been thumbed and turned so many hundreds of times. It had been her book, and she'd had it all her life.

"The book was about a very religious Christian man trying to make his way in a world full of troubles and problems. I won't tell you the whole story, it's too long. But I always remember, when he was confused and didn't know how to act, or what was the right thing to say, he'd ask himself, 'What would Jesus do?'

"See, he knew Jesus had doubts, too. But Jesus stuck to what he thought was the right thing to do. He was afraid sometimes, but he tried to be brave. And I'll bet that the people around him, including some of his followers, tried to convince him he was being foolish, getting in trouble with the Sanhedrin and the Romans."

Iris sat up in her chair, a sad smile playing across her face. "No, son, I'm not saying I'm like Jesus. Nobody is. But he inspires me sometimes. I'm doing this because I'm absolutely, totally certain that it's right. And if I didn't fight for what's right, if I didn't oppose what's happening to our land, I couldn't look at my own face in the mirror. I could never tell you to do what's right.

"See? That's what I mean. In the long run, it's really simple. You asked me why I have to do this. That's the answer."

"Yeah, I see, Mom. But there are a lot of people who disagree with you, aren't there? Like the government, a lot of people in town, your own brother. And your own son."

"Maybe they — and you — do, Bryan," she said, her voice quavering. "All I can do, I guess, is hope you can at least respect what I'm doing."

"Mom, to be honest, I'm not sure I can."

The phone rang. "I'll get it," Iris said.

Bryan watched his mother, wondering when was the last time they had received good news on the phone. Her back to him, Iris listened, and her shoulders slumped. She slammed down the receiver.

"I've been fired."

"Oh, God, Mom. Why?"

"That was Parker. He said he doesn't want me working in the store any more. He told me he doesn't want a jailbird — he actually used that word — working in his supermarket."

She sat down again and buried her face in her trembling hands.

Bryan wanted to comfort her, to embrace her and tell her everything would be all right. But he stayed where he was, watching her cry.

# FIVE

Bryan came into the kitchen the next morning to find the usual note from his mother on the table. He jammed his T-shirt tail into his shorts and got to work.

Kevin and Otto roused themselves about ten o'clock. I guess a pre-dawn trip to the ecological trenches would be too much for them today, Bryan mused. The two men devoured eight eggs, a pound of bacon and six slices of toast before they shouldered their packs and took off. Wonder if they have their camera this time, Bryan thought.

He was finishing up the dishes when Ellen burst in and threw herself into a chair. Her eyes were puffy, her hair messy, and anger flashed in her green eyes.

"My parents told me I can't see you any more!" she cried.

Bryan, as calmly as he could, folded the towel and hung it on the rack under the kitchen sink.

"My mother," he said.

"Yeah."

"Damn her, anyway!"

"Oh, don't blame her, Bry. Mom and Dad are being pigs about this."

"What did they say?"

"It doesn't matter. A lot of stupid stuff."

Sitting down opposite Ellen, Bryan said, "So what do we do now?"

Ellen swept her hair back. "Run away and join the circus?" She laughed hollowly. "Become street kids in Vancouver and get our faces on a milk carton?"

"Too bad a person couldn't trade in their parents like an old car," Bryan said.

"I don't know. Mine have too many miles on them. I wouldn't get much on a trade. One thing, though," she said, serious again. "I'm not going to stop seeing you, Bry."

He let his breath out slowly. "Good."

"So don't look so sad," Ellen said after a few moments.

"It isn't just that," he said. "Mom was fired last night. Her boss says he doesn't want her to work for him because of her arrest and that."

"Oh, Bryan. Your poor mother."

"Poor is right. No job, no pay. No allowance for me. Lucky we still have the two boarders for the time being. My mother," he finished.

When Bryan and Ellen found him walking up and down the hall in the hospital, Jimmy was humming a country-western tune — what he called hurtin' music — looking caged and bored. His left arm, encased in a plaster cast, was supported across his chest by a cloth sling. His face was discoloured and swollen, and an ugly red scrape marked his skin from chin to ear. He told them he was okay, doing fine, chasing nurses and looking forward to coming home the next day. Bryan heard the false cheer in his uncle's voice.

Ellen and Bryan picked up a couple of hamburgers and some fries on the way home, planning to nuke them in the microwave and watch a couple of game shows or laugh at the soaps that afternoon. As they walked down Bryan's driveway, Ellen pointed to something lying on the damp ground.

"Hey, what's that?"

Bryan picked up the object, brushing the damp earth from it. "It's a wallet."

"Brilliant deduction, Sherlock. Open it up."

Pinched under a stiff steel clip was a thick sheaf of money. "Wow," Bryan said, riffling the folded bills. He pulled out the driver's licence. "It's Otto's," he said.

"One of your guests?"

"Yeah. And this is a B.C. licence."

"Well, Sherlock, this is beautiful British Columbia."

"But Kevin and Otto told me they were from Toronto. Said they drove all the way out here to take part in the protests."

Crushing the paper sack of food between them as she leaned toward him, Ellen peered at the licence. "It's a

Vancouver address," she said. "Why would they lie to you?"

"I don't know, and I'm not going to ask." Bryan dropped the wallet at the basement door. "He'll find it easy enough here."

"Why not give it to him? Then you can ask him about the licence."

"Because I don't really care. It's none of my business anyway."

They zapped the burgers and fries and settled down on the couch. All through the episode of "Gilligan's Island" Bryan turned over in his mind the mystery of the driver's licence. What would be the point of Kevin's telling him they were from Toronto? And of putting Ontario plates on their van? Maybe he had misunderstood Kevin. Maybe he had bought the van in Ontario and hadn't changed the registration yet. Maybe —

"I know!" he half shouted.

Ellen jumped, spilling fries on her Madonna T-shirt. "You know what?" she asked. "How those dopes are going to get off Gilligan's Island?"

"No, I've solved the mystery. No wonder you call me Sherlock. I'm brilliant, Watson. Kevin must be the one from Ontario. It's his van, see?"

"Makes sense."

"Still, I was sure Kevin said 'we.' Oh, well. Any fries left?"

"No, you ate them all, Mr Oink."

"I ate them? You —"

"Hey, look, a news bulletin." Ellen pointed at the screen.

A bored-looking man in a cheap suit appeared where Gilligan had been seconds before. "Another act of sabotage," he intoned, "against Mackenzie Forest Industries in Orca Sound region. Details at six."

He disappeared, replaced by a commercial for toilet paper.

"Hey, Bryan," Jimmy said as he limped through the kitchen door. With his plastered arm in a sling, one side of his face purple and yellow and stitches puckering the shaved skin above the opposite temple, Bryan's uncle looked as though some malicious logging machine had tried to remove the left side of his body.

"Hey, Uncle Jimmy. How are you?"

"Not bad for somebody who lost a fight with a Sitka spruce bigger round than I am tall."

"So the tree wasn't very big, then," Bryan joked. "How about some coffee?"

Jimmy laughed. "Thought you'd never ask," he said, lowering himself carefully into a chair so as to keep his bad leg as straight as possible.

Bryan's mother came in a moment later, toting Jimmy's small suitcase and several cloth bags.

"Well," Jimmy said when Bryan had stowed his bear in his room and returned to the kitchen, "you still make the best coffee in Nootka Harbour, Bryan. Glad to have me back?"

"You bet."

"You don't look overly joyful to me." Jimmy had always been good at reading Bryan's moods.

"He's mad at his mom," Iris put in, stirring her coffee.

"Ellen's parents don't want her to see me any more," Bryan said.

"Who the hell do they think *they* are, the snotty buggers?" Jimmy exclaimed. "Mr Three-Piece-Suit in a Buick, and Mrs I'm-a-Big-Shot-Lawyer! You aren't good enough for them, I suppose!"

"Well, it's not exactly that," Bryan answered, sorry that he had brought it up.

Iris stared into her cup.

"So what's the problem?" Jimmy demanded.

In the silence, Jimmy looked at Bryan, at his sister, at his nephew again. "Ah," he said, nodding his head.

Iris fiddled with the sugar spoon.

"Well, well," Jimmy said quietly, "this here logging issue has sure done some mean work in this family." He struggled to his feet. "I'm kinda tired," he said. "Time to take my pills and hit the sack."

"Me, too," Iris said. Before she left the room she looked at Bryan. She left without saying anything.

Bryan cleared away the coffee mugs, turned off the light and went to his room. He wasn't tired, and he knew he would not be able to sleep. Putting on his earphones, he turned up the radio and lay down on his bed in the dark. He listened to a few tunes, then six or seven commercials. The news came on at the top of the hour.

When he heard the lead story, Bryan tore off the earphones and hurled them across the room.

There had been a third act of sabotage. This time, an abandoned trailer near one of the old clear-cuts had been burned down.

"Satisfied, Mom?" Bryan said in the darkness.

# SIX

Bryan's town did not have a courthouse. Not that the little community was without its share of drunks, brawlers, petty thieves and other bad actors of varying degrees of venality: there just weren't enough of them to deserve a whole building dedicated to their readjustment to society. So, Nootka Harbour generally sent its bad guys down to Victoria to stand before a judge.

The province considered the notion of searching out a temporary local venue to deal with the Orca Sound anti-logging protesters, because there were so many of them. The question was, where in Nootka Harbour to hold the trial?

The cop shop, as Elias referred to the place where his brother Zeke worked, had no room big enough. The hotel down by the harbour did, but the officials allowed that holding a trial in the room beside a dingy and smoky drinking hole — called the Rainbow Room — would not seem dignified. The library reading room certainly possessed stature, but the librarian had recently set up an extensive display of characters from famous children's stories, and the presence of large yellow duckies, white goosies, red foxes and at least one comical green dinosaur would, it was felt, detract from the gravity of the proceedings. The result of these deliberations was that when the long arm of the law drew Iris Troupe and the others to its bosom, the Talbot Inlet Community Centre meeting room was the place to be.

Ellen, Elias and Bryan planned to attend the trial, but Ellen called early that morning to tell Bryan that she had been grounded for going over to his house against her parents' wishes. Bryan and Elias arrived at the community centre at one o'clock, pushed their bikes through the crowded parking lot, and locked them to the pipe railing that stretched across the front of the building. Earning quite a few irritated stares, they shouldered their way through the onlookers to the doors, which were jammed open by bodies and guarded by a cop who looked like he'd already had a bad day. Bryan did not recognize the cop — probably, he thought, one of the many police brought in from other towns to police the demonstrations that now occurred every day except weekends, when MFI suspended its logging. The cop would not let the two friends in.

"His mom is one of the people on trial," Elias explained as Bryan stood by, embarrassed.

"Son, you have no idea how many times I've heard that same line today," the cop answered, pushing back his cap and mopping his broad forehead with a damp handkerchief.

"Show him your I.D., Bry."

Bryan fished his school activities card from his wallet and showed it to the cop.

"No good," he said. "I got no list of defendants to check that against, see? You could be anybody. There's nothing to prove your mom is in there at all."

Elias asked, "Have you considered believing us?"

This remark won no points with the cop. Elias nevertheless kept up a constant stream of babble as Bryan stood quiet, looking around, hoping no one who knew him was within earshot. After ten minutes of pressure from Elias, the cop gave in and let them by.

"Thanks for your help, there, Bry," Elias commented.

It took another few minutes of arguing to get through the doors of the meeting room, which was packed with spectators sitting on folding chairs. On one side, reporters were jammed together, jotting on steno pads, and looking hot and irritable. On the other, about two dozen men, women and children sat in glum silence. Behind a small table a woman in a suit was making notes on a long yellow pad. Probably the lawyer hired by the Save Orca Sound Legal Defence Fund, Bryan thought.

"We're just in time," Elias whispered.

As Bryan took up a position behind the last row of seated spectators, his mother rose and stood before the judge. Bryan almost didn't recognize her. She wore a floral-patterned dress and her normally casual hair was held neatly in place at her neck with a barrette.

The judge, a tall man with wire-rimmed glasses, sat

behind a file-strewn trestle table. He looked imposing even without the black robe and wig that Bryan had expected to see. He also sounded imposing. He began by telling Iris in a deep voice that she and her fellow activists had not convinced him that they acted from conscience. Rather, he intoned, they had displayed an illegal public tantrum for which there was no excuse.

Oh, oh, thought Bryan as he saw his mother set her shoulders. He recognized the gesture.

The judge went on to tell Iris that, as a family woman and a business person in the community, she should be the first person to obey the law, not one of the first to break it. She ought to be a responsible mother, providing a positive example for her child. He fined her five hundred dollars, warned her against any further action against the injunction, and asked her if she had anything to say.

That, Bryan thought, was a mistake. He braced himself, suddenly wishing he had not come.

For a small woman, Iris had no trouble making herself heard in the crowded room. She told the judge that *he* ought to be ashamed of *himself* for punishing with such large fines citizens who were, whether *he* thought so or not, acting according to their conscience. He also had an obligation to provide a positive example for the community by showing understanding and leniency to his fellow citizens, who, after all, were not embezzlers or murders but men and women — *and* children, she added with a degree of sarcasm that would have made Elias proud — who were trying to protect their environment from cynical commercial rape. Since he had seen fit to tell her what her duty was, she would like to suggest to His Honour that *his* duty was to serve his fellow citizens, not the multinational corporations at the root of all the trouble.

And that was when the judge interrupted her. "Mrs Troupe," he warned, without the objective calm that had marked his remarks so far, "my court will not brook disrespect. I advise you to desist and sit down. Your fine is increased to one thousand dollars, and if I hear another sarcastic word escape your lips I'll find you in contempt and throw you in jail!"

"Find her in contempt?" Elias hissed. "He couldn't find his ass with both hands and a compass."

Bryan was convinced he was so red with embarrassment he must have glowed like a light bulb. He glanced around, wishing he could disappear.

"Let's get out of here," he whispered.

"Not yet."

Moments later, the defendants, followed by their lawyer, filed down the centre aisle amid the murmur of the spectators. As Iris passed him, a look of surprise crossed her face. She smiled and shrugged her shoulders.

"I'll be home later, dear," she whispered. "I have a meeting."

"Nice going, Mrs Troupe," Elias said.

Bryan remained silent as he watched her leave.

When he got home, Bryan reported the courtroom proceedings to Jimmy, who burst into laughter at Iris taking on the judge — "That's my big sister!" he crowed — then called Ellen to tell her the news. As soon as she answered, he knew something was wrong. She was crying.

"Bry," she choked, "they're sending me away!"

"Away? Why? Where?"

"To my aunt's in Nanaimo. They're furious at me because I ignored their orders not to see you. They say you're . . ."

"I'm what?" he said bitterly. "The son of a jailbird or something?"

"That you're a bad influence on me, and a lot of other stupid stuff. It's not your mother, really. They don't like what she's doing, no, but it's me they're angry at. I've never disobeyed them before and they went completely mental. They yelled at me! They never yell at me. We're leaving today!" she wailed.

"I'll be right over," Bryan said. "Don't let them take you until I get there."

As if possessed, Bryan jumped on his bike and tore across town. Ellen's place was on the Gray's Passage side of the peninsula, in an area of large houses on spacious, thickly treed lots near the water. As he rode up the Thomsons' driveway, Bryan saw the three of them at the car.

Ellen's father, still in his suit, was putting suitcases into the trunk of the Buick. Her mother, her arms crossed on her chest, stood next to the car. When she caught sight of Bryan, Ellen ran down the drive to cut him off.

He stopped and dropped his bike, chest heaving. He was speechless. He had rushed to Ellen's house with no thought about what to do when he got there.

"I made it in time," he said.

"We're leaving now." Ellen's eyes were puffed from crying.

Bryan fought to keep his voice from cracking. "How long?"

"They want me to stay at my aunt's for the summer. They say I'll have a good time in Nanaimo." She rolled her eyes. "They say there's nothing to do around here in the summer anyway." Ellen shrugged, as if to say the idiocy of parents is beyond comprehension.

Bryan was aware of an ache in his throat and a hollow feeling in his chest. His fists opened and closed. "I guess we can't do anything about this."

Ellen forced a smile. "We could run away together."

"Yeah. Live in the bush and eat slugs while we sit around a campfire."

"Right. Wrestle bears and run with the deer."

"Build a log cabin."

"Oh, Bryan." She began to cry softly, and Bryan put his arms around her, drawing her fiercely against him. She buried her face in his chest. He looked up. Ellen's parents, standing side by side, looked back at him. His mouth set in a firm line, he tried to stare them down.

They won.

# SEVEN

Although he swore he needed his nephew to help him shift gears, Bryan suspected that Jimmy had asked him to come along to the meeting to take his mind off Ellen.

"What meeting?" he had asked.

"Well, my foreman wants me to come to a meeting over in Talbot Inlet. Something about a community group."

Bryan had immediately been suspicious. His uncle was probably the last person on the planet to be interested in joining any group, unless it was organized around the dart board at the hotel, but he decided to go along anyway, just to keep Jimmy company. His uncle had even dressed up for the occasion in a white shirt with his favourite bolo tie — a raven's head carved in pewter — clean jeans and polished cowboy boots. They left Iris bent over the fax machine, programming it to send out long-distance faxes during the night when the rates were low, and went out into a light drizzle.

Bryan knew that the logo on the truck's rusted front

quarter panel read "V8," but Jimmy claimed there were only six working pistons, one doubtful, and one just going around for the ride. Jimmy turned the ignition key, uttering a prayer that was only slightly sacrilegious. The twelve-year-old engine burped once, laid down a smoky backfire and rumbled to life.

The meeting was held in the community centre, in the same room where Iris had recently told off the judge. Already the brightly lit room was active. About thirty men and women milled around, talking and drinking from white plastic cups. Bryan noted the trestle tables laden with aluminum beer kegs, bottles of wine and platters of sandwiches cut into dainty quarters with no crust. In the centre of one table a huge smoked sockeye rested in a bed of lettuce, surrounded by cracked Dungeness crabs.

Jimmy let out a low whistle. "Wonder who sprung for all these goodies ?"

They stood uneasily in the centre of the room, neither of them comfortable in large gatherings. Bryan was already sorry he had come.

"Go on over there and grab some of that food, Bry, before it all goes bad."

"Hey, Jimmy! Glad you could make it."

They turned to see a man with a ruddy complexion bearing down on them, a foam-topped cup in one hand and a sandwich in the other.

"Hi, Scotty," Jimmy greeted him. "How's it goin'? Bryan, meet Scott Weatherby, my foreman."

The big man's blue blazer stretched tight across powerful shoulders when he shook hands.

"Good turnout tonight, eh, Jimmy? Let's get you a beer. Bryan, help yourself. I know you young fellas have a hollow leg."

A hollow leg? Bryan thought resentfully as he left them. He piled a few sandwiches on a foam plate, careful to avoid the ones made with chopped egg or the salmon salad. He took a cola from a tub of ice.

He scanned the crowd. They were working people, and some of them he recognized from around town. He was the only kid in the room. Great, he thought, hoping Jimmy would soon get bored and offer to leave. With nothing to do, he rejoined his uncle, who stood with a beer in hand, talking to Scott Weatherby.

". . . probably wondering what this is all about," Weatherby was saying.

"Yeah."

Noticing Bryan, the foreman asked, "Uh, can you excuse us for a minute, Bryan?"

Bryan's face flushed. "Sorry." He turned away.

"No, stay here, Bry," Jimmy said. Then to Weatherby, "He's all right, Scotty."

"Well," the big man went on, "we're going to start up a chapter of SAVE here in Talbot Inlet, and I figured you'd want to get in on it."

"SAVE?" Jimmy's brow creased, emphasizing the jagged line of his stitched wound.

"Yup. There's chapters all over the province now.

See, a lot of us in town figure that in all this controversy about logging the sound, the average man, like you and me, hasn't got no voice. I mean, we hear a lot of noise from the politicians, the corporations and the radicals — er" — he looked at Bryan — "the activists — no disrespect for your mom intended there, Bryan. They're in the papers and on TV all the time. Can't get away from them." He pushed the remains of a sandwich into his mouth and talked while he chewed. "But where's the ordinary citizen at? Who's speaking for us?" He took a swallow from his cup of beer.

"I see what you mean," Jimmy said.

So do I, thought Bryan, although he wondered, if his mother wasn't an ordinary citizen, who was?

"Don't get me wrong, Jimmy," Weatherby continued, as if reading Bryan's thoughts, "I'm not bad-mouthing people like Iris. I disagree with her, of course, and to tell you the gods' honest truth I wish her and her group would cease and desist, but she's got a right to her opinion. It's just that us people, you and me, who work in the bush and make our living from the bush, we don't have nobody speaking for us. See what I mean?"

Jimmy nodded. "That's for damn sure."

"SAVE organized the counter-demonstration out at the Big Bear not long ago." Weatherby said, beaming.

"I didn't know that."

"Yup, came up with the yellow ribbon idea, too." He grinned. "We even got a theme song."

Bryan now felt like a spy. His throat went dry and his

interest in the four sandwiches remaining on his plate suddenly evaporated. Did Scotty know that Bryan had been at the demonstration, when Iris had been arrested that day? He gulped down some of his cola and began to edge away.

"Come on," Weatherby said cheerfully, "there's somebody I want you to meet. You come, too, Bryan. You'll both like this guy."

He led them across the room to a small group of men gathered around one of the beer kegs.

"Charlie," Weatherby addressed a man who, dressed in a suit and tie, looked out of place in the group. "Meet a good friend of mine. Charlie Tanaka, Jimmy Lormer and Bryan Troupe."

Good friend? wondered Bryan. Tanaka's hand was smooth as he shook with Bryan. He hasn't cut too many trees lately, Bryan thought.

"Hello, Jimmy. How's the arm?" Tanaka said.

"Fine, fine."

"Glad to hear it."

"You're not from around here, are you?" Jimmy asked.

"Born in Delta. My parents still operate a small farm there. Scotty here has told me a lot about you."

"He has?"

Bryan wondered how Weatherby could have told Tanaka much, since he hardly knew his uncle. He looked at Jimmy and decided his uncle was riding this out to see where it would lead.

"Did Scotty fill you in on what's happening here

tonight?" Tanaka asked.

"Sort of."

"Well, a number of communities here on the island — Port Albert and Nanaimo, to name two — have established SAVE chapters so that citizens who depend on the forestry for their livelihood have a voice. We know that on this side of the island there are a few communities that are beset by the activists, and nobody is asking *their* opinion. Right now, the noise is all coming from one place. We want to, as it were, even the scales, to make sure the public gets a balanced view. That's the key word here," Tanaka emphasized, smiling. "Balance."

"I see."

Tanaka's calm voice was convincing. He's right, Bryan thought, but things are sort of "balanced" at Norm's B&B too, and it still isn't a lot of fun living there right now.

"Uh-huh," Jimmy said. "You're right. Nothing wrong with balance. I mean, everybody ought to be heard, I guess."

"Scotty here suggested, and I wholeheartedly agree," Tanaka went on, "that you'd be the perfect man to head up the Talbot Inlet chapter of SAVE."

Jimmy flushed. "Me?"

"Who's better qualified?" Scotty spoke up. "You've worked in the bush all your life. You were injured in the line of duty."

The line of duty? Bryan thought.

Jimmy looked down into his cup of beer. "Well . . . I

don't know if I'd have the time. I could help out, sure, I could give you an hour or so a day, but . . ."

Bryan knew that his uncle was a man who felt at home in his own sphere. Give him a job to do with his hands and he was full of confidence and purpose. But outside his realm, he lost all composure. Confronted by a person with education or wealth or power, Jimmy headed the other way.

"Oh," Tanaka said almost casually, "this would take a bit more of your time than that." He smiled again. Bryan realized Tanaka could turn the smile on and off at will.

"Then I don't see . . . ," Jimmy stumbled. "I mean, I gotta look for work. If I can't find anything here, I figured I'd try Nanaimo, so —"

"That's just it," Scotty said. "You get a salary, Jimmy. You wouldn't have to look for work no more. Which, if you don't mind my saying, you might have some trouble getting a job, what with your arm and all."

"A salary? This is a paying position?"

Bryan could guess at what was going on in his uncle's head. His humiliation at being out of work once more — even if it was an injury that caused his unemployment — struggling with his self-consciousness about accepting a job that might require paperwork, talking to people on the phone, organizing.

Turning on the smile once again, Tanaka put his hand on Jimmy's shoulder. "Yes, it is, Jimmy. You'd be the chairman. You'd be in charge."

Jimmy was silent. He tipped up his cup and drained

it, wiping the wisp of foam from his upper lip.

"Here, let me fill that up for you, Mr Chairman," Scotty said, taking the cup.

"Do you mind if I ask how much you were earning before you got hurt?" Tanaka asked.

Bryan could see the invisible weight rising from Jimmy's shoulders. A job. No more depending on his sister. Maybe turn that damn truck in on a newer model, one with an engine that didn't sound like someone was shaking a can of nails. His uncle told Tanaka his wage.

"I daresay we could match that."

"That's very generous." Bryan could hear the surprise in Jimmy's voice.

"Not at all. We need someone like you. What do you say? Willing to give it a try?"

"Yeah, I . . . uh, I could try it. See if I could manage."

"Wonderful."

Scotty handed Jimmy a brimming cup.

"There's just one thing, Jimmy," Tanaka said. "If you were to take this job on, would you be living in the same place?"

"The same place?" Jimmy looked at Scotty, then back to Tanaka. The two men waited.

"He means," Bryan said stiffly, "would you still be living with Mom."

"You understand," Scotty said hastily, scowling at Bryan, "it's nothing against Iris, Jimmy. Like I said earlier, I — we — respect her point of view and all —"

"Of course we do," Tanaka said smoothly.

"Well," Jimmy faltered. "I was sort of planning to get a place of my own, anyway, soon as I could put some cash together."

"If you need a little advance, that's no problem," Tanaka said. "We'll supply any office equipment you might need, secretarial assistance, and of course we'd cover your phone bill."

"Well . . . I guess . . . sure, that sounds great."

"Fine, fine," Tanaka urged. "I'm delighted you'll be joining us. The more men like you, the better the Talbot Inlet chapter of SAVE will be."

Scotty patted Jimmy on the back. "Good man, Jimmy. This is great. Isn't this great, Charlie ?"

"Thanks, Mr. Tanaka. I really appreciate this," Jimmy said with more feeling than Bryan had heard in his voice for a long time.

Smiling one last time, Tanaka looked at his gold watch. "And now, if you'll forgive me, gentlemen, I've got to be on my way. Promises to keep, and all that." He shook Jimmy's hand, then Scotty's, then Bryan's. "Gentlemen, it's been a pleasure. I'll be in touch, Jimmy. Oh, by the way, we'll start your pay as of last Monday, if that's all right."

On the way home, Jimmy whistled country-western tunes and banged rhythmically on the ancient steering wheel. Beside him, Bryan stared ahead into the intersecting yellow circles cast by the headlights. He didn't know what to make of what had transpired at the Talbot Inlet Community Centre, but he knew that whatever it vas, it was taking someone else away from him.

At the dinner table the next day, Jimmy said with what Bryan knew was false cheer, "Iris, it's time for me to move out."

Iris's jaw dropped.

"Got a flat over on Anne Street," Jimmy went on, looking sheepish. "You know that big two-storey, couple named Smolka own it?"

"Yes, I know it. Jimmy, why not stay here? You don't have to move out."

Bryan remained silent. He had promised his uncle he would not tell Iris that Jimmy had a new job until he had moved. "It'll hurt her feelings if she thinks I'm leaving because of her and her committee," he had said. "I'll tell her a few days after I'm set up."

Jimmy mopped up some gravy with a piece of roll and popped it into his mouth. "You know I never planned to stay here, Iris. I just needed a place until I got my feet back under me. Anyway," he said, rising, "I'm gonna do some packing up. I'll take my stuff over there tomorrow."

Bryan followed Jimmy to his room and sat on the bed while Jimmy transferred clothes from the closet to a beat-up suitcase resting on a chair. His battered face seemed tight and drawn.

"Do you have to go?" Bryan finally said. "Won't they let you take the job anyway?"

Jimmy stopped, a few worn shirts clutched in his rough hand. The collars were frayed and the pocket had been torn off one of the shirts, leaving a dark patch of the faded cloth.

"We'll still see each other a lot, don't worry."

"Yeah, but it won't be the same."

Jimmy lay the shirts in the suitcase, then began pulling rolled-up socks from his dresser. "We'll have some good times, don't you worry. I'm only across town."

"It's Mom, isn't it?" Bryan asked him. "It's her and her stupid committee of tree-huggers. That's why Tanaka wants you to move."

"It's more like I don't want to be a burden, Bryan. I'm workin' again, so I can afford to have my own place. I want to get back on my feet, like I told your mom. I would have moved anyway if I didn't get hurt. I don't like to be a burden."

"But you're not."

"That's real nice of you to say —"

"But it's true."

"But I feel like I am, I guess. I just feel better on my own. More independent."

"Well, I think you're being stupid!" Bryan shouted and ran out of the room.

"Bryan!" his mother called from the kitchen. "Time to do the dishes."

"Do them yourself!" he yelled back, and slammed his bedroom door.

"What was *that* all about?" Iris asked a while later. She had knocked on his door and wouldn't go away when Bryan told her to.

When she came in he was lying on his bed with the pillow over his head.

"I can't hear you," she said.

"I didn't say anything."

"What?"

Exasperated, Bryan threw off the pillow and sat up, jammed into the corner where his bed met the wall. "I *said* I didn't *say* anything."

His mother was sitting in his desk chair. "Gotcha!" She smiled. She had on one of her track suits that Bryan hated. They made her look dumpy. And poor.

"Very funny, Mom."

"So what's the reason for the rudeness? That's not like you."

"Jimmy's leaving because of you," he almost shouted. "You and that stupid damn committee."

She ran his fingers through her hair. "I don't think so, Bryan. Of course, I know he doesn't agree with what I'm doing —"

"That's for sure!"

"Is that what Jimmy told you? That he's moving out because of me?"

"No, he said that *wasn't* the reason. But I don't believe him. I happen to know it's true." Bryan could not bring himself to tell his mother that Jimmy had a job with a very big string attached.

"Believe him, son. Jimmy doesn't hold back on things. He'll always tell you the truth, even if it hurts you. That's the kind of man he is. It's one of the things I admire about him."

Bryan remembered a time a year or so back when Iris was going out to some church meeting. She had come into the kitchen and asked Jimmy and her son how she looked. Bryan told her she looked fine in her jeans and bush shirt. She looked like she always looked, as far as he was concerned. Jimmy had said, "You look like you just walked out of the bush. Wear a dress, Iris. You're a nice-lookin' woman. Show it off a little." Iris had been angry and pleased at the same time.

"I guess you're right," he said, knowing that, this one time, Jimmy had not told his sister everything. No matter how much he disliked what Iris was doing about the logging issue, he would not hurt her.

"I wish he wasn't going, though," Bryan said.

After his mother left him alone, he wondered how many more people he cared about would be pushed out of his life because of a bunch of old trees.

# EIGHT

Bryan hopped on his bike and headed south on the shore road, pedalling fast down the tunnel of shade cast by the conifers that lined the blacktop. When the road veered sharply west, he turned in the opposite direction into the trees, along a path that soon took him to the beach. He dismounted and shoved his bike into a copse of young hemlock, out of sight. Only a few paces farther on, he broke from the cool of the trees and into the sunlight. He waded through waist-high grass and onto the open sand.

The beach ran untroubled for kilometres in each direction. To his left, the sand curved westerly, fringed with conifers that hid a few houses from view. Whitecapped breakers rolled in, crashing fifty metres from the strand. The colourful wetsuits of a few surfers winked in and out of sight. In the distance the surf thundered against grey-black cliffs, tossing clouds of spume into the sky. To Bryan's right, the waves that curled into the bay were flatter and less powerful, their energy dissipated long before they hissed up the sand. Overhead an osprey wheeled, waiting.

He sat down on a bleached log that had been embedded in the sand years before, and looked out to sea where, about three hundred metres off shore, a low rocky island sustained no more than a dozen wind-beaten pines. At low tide, Bryan would sometimes walk to the island and look out over the limitless expanse of the Pacific and feel the salt wind on his face. But now, when he could sit on his log and watch the tide coming in, now was the time he liked best. The spit of sand between him and the island gradually diminished as the sea swept in from both east and west, losing its power as it encircled the island to meet just in front of him. He didn't know how the water could move from opposite directions to come together in this place and at the same time creep toward the shore. It fascinated him.

Bryan was aware that, if he put the problem to Ellen, she would come here with a thick sheaf of tidal tables, wind and weather patterns, charts of the ocean bottom and textbooks about the sea. She would offer a neat explanation that would satisfy a scientist. Elias would give him a quizzical who-really-cares look. Walter, if he came here at all, would stand ankle-deep in the rising wavelets and say little or nothing because, to him, silence was the best answer and mysteries did not need to be explained.

Bryan did not want to solve the mystery. He knew that many people had a place that they went to when hey wanted to escape or think or grieve. This was his place. He had shared it with no one, not even Ellen, not because it was a secret — many people from town used his beach — but because he knew he could not begin to explain its attraction for him, no more than he could, years ago in Drumheller, explain why sometimes he would climb the crumbling banks of the Badlands just to feel the prairie breeze on his skin. In this place the wind, the sea and the land were always present and never the same. Sometimes in summer the sky was blue and porcelain hard, the sand blindingly white, the dark rocks etched against the waves, the wind sighing through the conifers. The next day might bring a scene of rain and muted greys, or a wind that drove thick mist shoreward.

Beneath the constant diversity there was something eternal, something as inexplicable and yet as real as the sea moving in opposite directions before him. It was this permanence that moved him in a way he could not put into words. Bryan wished with his whole heart that there was a corresponding permanence in his own life, as he was gripped by the fear that his world was slipping away from him. The way it had once before.

# NINE

Bryan slept fitfully all through that night — thinking about Ellen and trying to figure out a way to get her back — until he awoke to see 4:28 on his clock radio. He dove beneath his pillow but remained awake until he got out of bed around six, grumpy and tired. Iris had gone out right after breakfast, but not before giving Bryan his marching orders for the day: wash the kitchen floor, vacuum and dust the living room. She didn't tell me when I had to start, Bryan thought as he turned on the TV and flicked from station to station, trying to find something un-stupid to watch.

Kevin and Otto thumped upstairs for breakfast. They made short work of the sausages, eggs and hashbrowns Bryan fried up for them. While he cleared the dishes and the two men had their second cup of coffee, Kevin asked for a favour.

"What is it?" Bryan asked over the rush of hot water into the sink.

"Well, Otto and I have a bit of laundry to do and we

wondered if you'd mind if we used your washer and dryer."

"I don't think Mom would go for that," he answered. "The B&B fee is for room and breakfast, that's all. Sorry. There's a twenty-four-hour laundromat pretty close to here," he added.

"We get along good with Iris, Bryan. I'm sure she'd agree. Besides, we're really whacked, you know? Long day at the Wasteland yesterday, right, Otto?"

Otto didn't reply.

"And besides, that laundromat is likely packed with tourists. From the campgrounds. It would really be a help if you could make an exception for this one time, Bryan. One hand washes the other, in a manner of speaking." He winked.

He's guilting me into it, Bryan thought. He helped me paint the fence and said that I didn't need to clean their rooms. So now he's calling in the favour. Bryan didn't ask how Kevin figured the laundromat would be packed at nine o'clock in the morning. And he didn't tell the men that their efforts at the protest site didn't gain any sympathy from him.

"Okay," he said over his shoulder. "But just this once. And you have to do it now, before Mom comes home."

After the two men cleared out of the kitchen Bryan dried the dishes and swept the kitchen floor. He lifted the chairs onto the table. As he descended the basement stairs to fetch the bucket and mop, he saw Otto in the laundry room, loading clothes into the washer. He was almost at the door of the tiny room, intending to ask Otto if he knew how to operate the machine, when the man looked up, saw him and pushed the door shut. Okay by me, Bryan thought.

He found the mop and bucket and returned to the kitchen. With a total absence of enthusiasm he washed the kitchen floor and then rapidly pushed the vacuum around the furniture in the living room. He took the dust rag and made a quick circuit of the room. The kitchen floor was still damp when he finished, so he tried the TV again.

One cartoon program and half a game show later, Bryan heard the door slam, then Kevin's van start up. He turned off the set and replaced the kitchen chairs around the table. He took the bucket and mop to the basement. The laundry room door was ajar and the light was still on.

"Otto, you still here?" he called out. "You finished in the laundry room?" No answer. "Kevin?" Silence.

Bryan tried the doors to the two bedrooms. Both were locked. He went into the laundry room to turn off the light. Mom will go ape if she finds this on, he thought. Then he noticed a curious odour in the warm, damp air. Mixed with the smell of soap and bleach was something he couldn't identify. He shrugged and reached for the pull string that hung from the light bulb — and caught sight of something grey sticking out from under the washer. He bent down and pulled it out. Otto must have dropped it, he thought. It was a thick woollen work sock.

And it smelled of kerosene.

Bryan quickly stuffed the sock back, his mind racing. He turned out the light, closed the door and sprinted upstairs. Then he cursed his stupidity. Otto would know he had been in the laundry room. He went back to the basement, turned the light back on and left the door open.

He went to the fridge, got a can of cola and took it into the living room. Instead of flicking on the TV, he sat in the bay window that looked out over Osprey Cove. High cumulus clouds floated like puffy islands in a sea of sky, and waves pushed lazily toward the rocks of the cove.

Bryan didn't know where Kevin had bought his van, or how he got the Ontario licence plates, but when he put together the fact that Otto's driver's permit was for British Columbia, that the two men had shown a reluctance to take their clothing to a public laundromat and that at least one article of that clothing smelled of kerosene, he could come to only one conclusion. Kevin and Otto were the saboteurs who had set fire to the MFI truck and burned down the trailer. And they were also responsible for the cops hassling his mother. He slammed the empty can onto the table.

The question was, what should he do about it?

Should he tell his mother? If he did, would they hurt her? If he told Zeke, would the cops assume that Iris, known to be a leader in the anti-logging demonstrations, owner of the house where Kevin and Otto were living, was a co-conspirator? Maybe, he thought, I should confront them myself and just tell them to clear out.

The phone rang. "Hello," he said.

"Hello yourself!"

"Ellen! Where are you? Are you back home? Can —"

"Slow down, Bry. I'm still at my aunt's."

"Oh."

"Still the snappy conversationalist, I see," she joked.

"Well, yeah. Haven't had much time to take lessons since you left. Although it seems like months."

"You're sweet," Ellen said. "But I bet you've already found another girlfriend."

"Yeah, right. They're lined up at the door. Nobody like you, though."

"I miss you, Bry."

"Me too."

"So," Ellen said, false cheer in her voice, "what's new?"

Bryan told her about Jimmy moving out and about his new job.

"Hmm."

"What?"

"Seems a little fishy, doesn't it? Makes you kind of wonder who's behind this SAVE outfit."

"Well, I thought it sounded a little too good to be true. And there's something else." Bryan told her about the sock.

"I think you're right. It sounds like those guys are trouble."

"What should I do?"

"Why not tell your mother? Maybe she can come up with some excuse to get them to leave. Like she booked the rooms before. Something like that."

"Good idea." Bryan pictured his mother's face when she found out that her two fellow activists and only source of income were a little *too* committed to the cause.

"But we should try to think of a way to make them stop," Ellen said.

Bryan told her his fear that if the men were caught it would reflect back on his mother.

"Good point," Ellen admitted.

"Hey!" Bryan cut in. "I just remembered. This is long-distance. Maybe you should get off the phone."

"Relax. My aunt told me to talk as long as I want. And guess what? She's a tree-hugger! She sent fifty bucks to the SOS defence fund."

"Oh, no," Bryan said, "another one."

When the sky was beginning to brighten the next morning, Bryan and Walter walked down to the docks, boarded Walter's boat and put out into Gray's Passage to check the crab traps. They sky was overcast, the wind cool but light. They spent the morning making the rounds, winching up the big wire-mesh traps, removing crab if there was any, rebaiting the traps and lowering them into the water again. In between sessions, they sipped coffee and watched the seabirds swing on the breeze, crying to one another.

Bryan tried to lose himself in his work, but he couldn't get his mind off the problem posed by Kevin and Otto. Something had to be done, he knew. And he knew just as well that whatever the "something" was, it probably had to be initiated by him. Without knowing why, he decided not to share his problem with Walter.

When they had tied the boat to the dock, they loaded three boxes of crabs onto a dolly and Bryan hauled them up the road to McGregor's Crab House, the little restaurant that always bought Walter's catch. Bryan took the money back to his neighbour, who by this time had made the boat tight and secure.

When they got back home, Bryan was surprised to find Jimmy there.

"Your mom's been arrested again," he said without so much as a hello. "And this time it don't look so good."

Bryan glanced at Walter. "What happened this time?" he asked his uncle.

"For some reason she decided to park her carcass on the bridge and block the trucks again. So she's broken the terms of her release. They already took her to Nanaimo. She could get six months this time. This is real serious."

Six months? Bryan took off his sweater and hurled it against the wall. Six months for sitting on a bridge? He didn't know who made him more furious, more tied in knots, his mother or the law.

# TEN

Bryan didn't bother with lunch, even though he was ravenous from the morning's slugging on the boat. It was raining lightly — what some residents of Nootka Harbour would call a heavy fog — when he set out for Elias's place on his bike.

The Wilsons' house was a big two-storey with a verandah stretched across the front. When Bryan arrived, breathless, he found Elias and Zeke rebuilding the steps. He knew Elias's dad liked to keep the place looking slick because of the art gallery he had made by knocking out a wall on the first floor and converting what had been a parlour and dining room. He displayed some of his paintings there.

Bryan was pleased to see Zeke at home — he still lived with Elias and his parents — because he wanted to talk to both of them. Working away despite the rain — in Nootka Harbour, if you postponed work — or anything else — because of rain, nothing would ever get done — they greeted him as he propped his bike against the verandah railing. The stair risers were in place and the brothers were measuring planks to cut the steps.

Zeke looked a little sheepish as he handled the tape measure, still embarrassed, Bryan thought, at having to arrest his mother.

"Hey, Zeke," he said, getting to the point right away, "do you mind if I ask you something about police work?"

"Feel free," the big man said. He was dark, like Elias, heavy across the shoulders, with a boyish face.

Elias picked up a handsaw. "Thinking of joining the boys in blue, Bry? I don't think you'd make the height restrictions."

Bryan gave Elias the finger and said to Zeke, "Well, suppose a person thought a couple of other persons were committing crimes and he was afraid to go to the cops because a different person might get into trouble if the two persons were breaking the law."

Zeke stood and brushed sawdust from his jeans. "Ah . . . "

Elias laughed. "You're starting to sound like Walter, Bry." He began to saw the plank, balancing it across the risers.

"Yeah, Bryan, that wasn't what you'd call clear and to the point," Zeke said.

"Okay." Bryan tried again, wondering if he should have even started. "Let's suppose —"

"Hang on a second," Elias said, interrupting his sawing, his tone serious. "I think what Bryan wants to do," he said, talking to his brother but looking at his friend, "is describe a totally imaginary situation to you. Just sort of for the fun of it. Right, Bry?"

"Right. Totally imaginary. Just for the fun of it. Because I'm interested in how a cop might see it."

"A cop who was on duty," Elias added. "Which you aren't, Zeke."

A wide grin formed on Zeke's face as he removed his baseball cap and scratched his head. "Nope, I'm off duty today. That's right. Off cop duty and on step-building duty." His grin faded. "But — and this is a big 'but' — if somebody was to know for certain that a serious crime had been committed, and if that somebody was to tell a real live cop, on duty or off, that cop would have to do something about it, because he's sworn to do so. Do you get my drift, Bryan?"

Not at all certain that he wanted to keep going on this, Bryan kept his mouth shut. Elias took up his sawing again, and Zeke sat down on the plank to keep it steady. Bryan kicked at the damp spruce needles beside the walk. Then the picture of his mom sitting in jail for half a year formed in his mind, and his confusion slowly turned into anger, anger at jerks like Kevin and Otto, sneaking into his town and into his life, causing havoc and taking off again, probably for some condo in Vancouver.

"Here's the imaginary situation," Bryan began once more. "There's this person who owns a B&B. This person is an activist who's been arrested for the second time —"

"Did you say *second*?" Elias interrupted.

"Not *first*?" Zeke asked.

"Second."

Abandoning his saw, Elias stood and listened.

"Now this person, let's say, has rented rooms to a couple of guys who claim they're from Toronto. They've got a van with Ontario plates. But one of them has a B.C. driver's licence and —"

"How do you know that?"

"He doesn't know anything, Zeke," Elias said. "This is just a theory, remember?"

"Okay, okay. Keep going, Bryan."

"So anyway, someone who knows this B&B person thinks that these two guys are responsible for some pretty serious vandalism that's been going on around a certain logging site. But he's afraid to go to the cops because they might come down on his mother — who he knows," Bryan said, no longer caring that he had stepped out of the imaginary situation and into real life, "had nothing to do with the vandalism. And he's afraid not to go to the cops, because things might get a lot worse and who can guess what would happen then?"

The three of them stood there in the drizzle.

"Let's go in the house and get something to drink," Zeke suggested.

In the family room, each of them holding a can of pop, Zeke continued.

"Okay, Bryan," he said quietly, "let's do it this way. I'm hearing some stuff, but I don't know where I heard it. Right?"

Bryan nodded, relieved. Until Zeke went on.

"But, like I said outside, if I find that someone has done something against the law, no matter who that person is and no matter how much I like and admire that person, I can't let it go. Now if you can handle that, keep talking, and drop this charade. If you can't, you can help Elias and me with them damn steps, and anything else — besides how to get the steps built — that we have talked about gets forgotten. And no harm done."

"I don't know what to do," Bryan said.

"Talk, Bryan," Elias told him. "Your mother just isn't the kind of person to get mixed up in sabotage, and everybody knows it. Right, big brother?"

Zeke waited. Bryan read the words on his pop can a few times, took a deep breath and told Zeke everything — the licence, the sock with kerosene, Kevin and Otto taking pictures at the Big Bear River the day Walter and Bryan were looking for Iris.

"You understand," Zeke said, "that you're not to pass on anything I say? Elias already knows this. I can't feel free to talk about my job if people go blabbing and gossiping around town, saying, 'Zeke Wilson said this and that.' Or I'd lose my job."

"I understand, Zeke."

"First, nobody on the job — at least, the locals — really thinks your mother is a saboteur. We had to investigate her and her group because it's routine — and because certain powerful interests around here put pressure on the force to do that. I happen to admire Iris, like I said outside. I agree with her goals, too. Elias and me are half-native, remember. But us cops gotta do our jobs without taking sides. Anyway, it sounds to me like the cops ought to take a hard look at those two guys staying at your house. I want you, when you get home, to call me when they're in so I can drive by and get their plate number. I'll put it through the computer. I'll put their names through, too. If I meet them on the road I'll pull them over and check their paperwork. I'll tell them we're looking for a stolen van. I don't want them to know I'm looking at them, see? Meantime, here's what I want you to do."

"What?" Bryan blurted, pleased at the prospect of finally being able to *do* something.

Zeke took a long pull from his can of cola. "Nothing."

"Huh?"

"Nothing. Leave it to me. You give those guys a wide berth. And in a day or so, if I find out something — or find out nothing, since these guys may be, probably are innocent — I'll tell you and Jimmy, and Jimmy can give them their walking papers."

"He'd love to do that anyway," Bryan said. "He doesn't like tree-huggers."

Elias spoke up. "But your Mom needs the money they bring in."

"Yeah, that's true."

"Well, if they're clean, you may want to let them stay," Zeke said. "That's up to you. So." He stood and held out his hand. "We got a deal?"

Bryan rose and shook with him. "Deal," he said,

relieved. "Thanks, Zeke."

"No problem. Now, I gotta get back to work. Don't we, little bro?"

"Yeah, yeah. What a slave-driver."

As Zeke walked down the hall to the front door, Elias held Bryan back.

"Are those two guys at home nights?"

"Usually. Why?"

"Days?"

"They're always out at the peace camp. They head out right after breakfast."

"Okay, call me tomorrow soon as they're gone."

"Eliaaaas!" came Zeke's wail from outside.

"Why? What's up?"

"Maybe we can do some investigating on our own."

# ELEVEN

Early the next morning, Bryan's mother phoned from jail in Nanaimo. She told him that the day started early there; as soon as the sun came up the women were herded down to breakfast, decked out in "these lovely blue dresses they make us wear."

"Are you okay, Mom?"

"Oh, sure," Iris answered with obviously false cheerfulness.

"So, what happened this time?"

"It's, well, hard to explain —"

"I mean," Bryan cut in, hoping he did not sound as angry as he felt, "you told the court you wouldn't demonstrate against the injunction, right?"

"Yes, but I felt I had to. I guess that's the simplest way to put it."

Bryan was on the verge of telling his mother that he had seen her carted away on her first arrest and that because she was a tree-hugger, she now had two crooks living in the house. But she wasn't there to deal with them. And because she was a tree-hugger, Jimmy had had to leave home, so he couldn't help either. And if it hadn't been for her, Ellen would still be in Nootka Harbour.

He wanted to tell her all these things. But he said nothing.

"I just couldn't stand there on the sidelines and watch the cops taking kids and seniors and university students and people from my own community without standing with them," Iris said.

"I understand what you want, Mom. At least I think I do. I just don't see why you have to go to jail for it." And screw up my life from top to bottom, he thought.

"Well, I may be home in a day or two. I can probably get out on bail. But the word is that they're going to put us to trial fast. Anyway, son, there's a line-up behind me for the payphone. I'll try and call you each morning around this time."

Bryan stared out across the cove, his mind a prickly batch of emotions. His anger at his mother honed a sharp edge of guilt when he thought of her alone in a jail, living with hard women who probably belonged there, cut off from her son and brother, her community and friends. He wanted to feel sympathy, to show her he was with her. But how, when he wasn't with her?

Bryan began to make breakfast for Kevin and Otto. They came upstairs when they smelled the coffee. Hoping that his suspicions did not show, he served them bacon and eggs with a platter of buttered toast, planning to make a quick exit from the kitchen.

But Kevin was in a talkative mood. He rambled on and on about the activities at the Big Bear River bridge and delivered a sermon on what a great woman Iris was. Finally, he wound himself down and asked, "So how's that girlfriend of yours? What's her name? Eleanor?"

"Ellen."

Otto smiled and forked a large gob of scrambled egg into his mouth. "She's more than okay. She's a nice little piece, that one."

Kevin shot his companion a hard look. "You sure are a fine cook, Bry," he said.

"That's Bryan to you. I've got some work to do." He thumped down the hall and slammed his bedroom door. No wonder Otto doesn't talk much, he thought. The guy's a pig.

Soon afterwards, the scrape of chairs and the bang of the kitchen door told Bryan the two men had gone. When he heard the van roar to life, he sneaked a look out his window, making sure that both men were leaving. Then he got on the phone to Elias.

Fifteen minutes later, Bryan's friend burst into the house, breathless from a bike ride at break-neck speed, wearing his green Pacific Sands Provincial Park shorts and shirt.

"We have to do this fast," Elias announced excitedly. "I have to be at work at ten-thirty."

"Do what? What's the plan?"

"We're going to toss their rooms."

"No, we're not. They lock their doors — I've checked before — and there are two keys to each room. They have one each and Mom has one of each on her key-chain, which is probably in a brown envelope with her name on it in a file cabinet in Nanaimo Minimum-Security Facility for Women."

"So we break in."

"No, we do not break in. Mom would kill me if we damaged the doors, and those two scumbags might be a little suspicious when they come home from a hard day on the protest line and find their bedroom doors splintered."

"Hey, Bry," Elias laughed, "I thought I was the sarcastic one. There's hope for you yet. Go get your student I.D."

"'Break-in' is just an expression," Elias gloated a minute later as he ran the thin plastic card between the door jamb and the lock of Kevin's room. The door swung open. Otto's door proved no more of a challenge.

"Well, Mr Expert," Bryan sneered, "do you think we might need a look-out? Or were you planning to say something really clever if the two guys come home early?"

His face flushed, Elias answered, "You're right. Go stand by the outside door and whistle if —"

"No chance. You stand guard."

Arguing was something Elias was good at, and he pulled out every trick he knew, but Bryan would not budge. Finally, Elias opened the basement door partway to get a good view of the driveway, then gave Bryan a dramatic nod and thumbs-up.

Bryan entered Kevin's bedroom first. The single be
was a disaster area — blankets strewn half on, half off th
bed, a pair of jeans tangled up in the mess. On the floc
socks and underwear. Two hardcore girlie mags on th
bedside table. "Jeez," Bryan said to himself as he replace
one of them on the table. On the pine dresser, a con
clutching a few long hairs, a half-empty bottle
whiskey, and two glasses that hadn't been washed late
resting in a cluster of ring marks on the wood.

Bryan pulled open the drawers one by one, searchir
among the jumbled clothing. Nothing. He knelt an
looked under the bed. As he rose, his eye caught th
white edge of an envelope just visible under the maga
zines. Carefully, he slipped it out. On the front wa
Kevin's name. The return address read "Mackenzi
Forest Industries."

Bryan drew out a single piece of paper. It was
cheque made out to Kyle Canning. And the cheque wa
issued by MFI.

It doesn't take a scholar, Bryan thought, to figure tha
Kyle Canning and Kevin Campbell are the same guy. H
slipped the envelope back into place and left the room

If Kevin's (or Kyle's) room was a zoo, Otto's was
monastery cell. A carefully made-up bed. Nothing o
the night table, nothing on the dresser top. Inside th
dresser, neatly folded clothes. On the floor next to th
dresser, a cellular phone resting in its recharger. A cam
era bag, zipped shut, on the floor beside the closet. Brya

opened the closet. Half a dozen shirts hung there. Beneath them, a leather briefcase.

Okay, Bryan whispered to himself, now we're getting someplace. After noting carefully the exact location of the briefcase in the closet, he lifted it to the bed. He pushed the catches. They flipped open with a satisfying click.

Inside was a roll of fax paper, dense with names and numbers. Again noting how it was situated in the briefcase — I could teach Elias a few things about burglary, Bryan thought — he placed it on the carpet beside him. Next came half a dozen file folders, which Bryan scanned quickly, learning nothing. He put them aside. Last, an envelope exactly like the one he had found in Kevin's room. It, too contained a cheque, made out to Oliver McCann, for a much higher amount.

Bryan replaced the envelope, then the file folders, and carefully unrolled the fax paper. When he began to read the names and telephone numbers his stomach lurched.

Startled by a whistle, Bryan jumped. The fax paper sprang back into a tight roll.

"Bryan!" Elias hissed. "They're back!"

Bryan slammed the briefcase shut and carefully put it back in exactly the same place. In half a second he was out of the bedroom, checking the doorknob to be sure it was locked. As he slipped past Kevin's door he depressed the inside knob and turned it, then closed the door.

Elias pushed the basement door shut. "They're

just outside! Quick!"

"No! Here," Bryan said, shoving his friend bodily into the laundry room. "We don't have time to go up. They'll hear us on the stairs!"

Bryan had just plunged them into darkness by closing the door to the laundry room when he heard the outside door open.

# TWELVE

The rain pelted against Bryan's face, driven by gusts of wind as he pedalled along the two-lane blacktop into the centre of town. The noon-hour shoppers and tourists leaned into the rainy wind, shoulders hunched, scurrying to get out of the downpour. Bryan skidded to a stop outside the cop shop, leaned his bike against a railing and dashed inside.

Elias had rushed off to work as soon as Bryan and he had emerged from the laundry room, blinking and momentarily blinded by the basement lights the two activists had, as usual, left burning. Otto and Kevin — or whatever their names were — had retrieved the cellular phone they had forgotten and had left, arguing about something.

Bryan had sat at his desk with a can of cola, shaking, mulling over the significance of his discoveries and attempting to control his fear and apprehension. So, Kevin and Otto were really Kyle and Oliver. That much was clear. Just as obvious was that, although Kevin/Kyle did most of the talking, Otto/Oliver was the pair's leader.

It was harder for Bryan to figure why MFI was writing cheques to them. Blackmail? Extortion — "Pay us or we'll blow up more trucks"? Would MFI buy off two jerks like them not to set fire to useless trucks or dilapidated trailers? Come on, Bryan, he had said to himself, you've been watching too many late-night movies.

No, he concluded, the two guests at Norm's B&B worked for Mackenzie Forest Industries. And if that was true, then his theory that they were the saboteurs seemed dead wrong. To think that Otto and Kevin would sabotage the property of the company they worked for seemed impossible.

Impossible until he thought about the most important piece of evidence, the one that had jolted him with fear and surprise as he was on his knees in Otto/Oliver's room: the roll of fax paper. Bryan had seen enough of the names and numbers listed in densely packed small print to realize that what he held in his hand was a print-out from the activity log — the stored list of all names and numbers of people who had sent or received a message — from the fax machine in his own family room.

Why would Otto/Oliver want that list? Bryan racked his brain, sipping his cola. Maybe Otto, personally, didn't. Maybe MFI did.

If Otto worked for MFI, he wasn't a tree-hugger. And if he wasn't a tree-hugger, he had to be a spy, a plant, an agent. A spy who took pictures of activists at the peace camp. A spy who was at the camp every day and would know every move the tree-huggers were making. And worst of all, a spy who set things on fire to make the SOS committee and its supporters look like a bunch of violent crazies — especially the chairperson, my mother.

Those bastards, he thought. They live in our house, pretend to be friends. Here, let me help you paint that fence, Bry. We really admire your mother. What crap. No wonder Mom doesn't trust the company. If they do this to people, what do they care about trees?

Once everything had fallen into place, he had hopped on his bike and set out in the rain.

The cop at the counter looked up Zeke's name in a roster. "He's on patrol out near the peace camp today," she told Bryan.

"Thanks. Can I use your phone?"

He placed a call and, when he got no answer, said "Thanks" once more, already in motion. Back into the rain. Back on the bike, aiming it toward the hotel.

The Rainbow Room was anything but a bright bow of colour. It was dark, smoky, furnished with small round tables and cheap hard-backed chairs. Cowboy music played in the background. In one corner, some guys were playing shuffleboard and hiking beer. At a large round table, others sat smoking and hiking beer. Jimmy stood to the side, one arm in a sling, aiming a dart while his opponent watched.

Bryan knew that, although Jimmy spent a lot of time in bars, he was not a heavy drinker. He had learned long ago that when alcohol took control of his brain it tapped into a dark pool of anger that propelled him into fights with men he did not know, over issues he could not remember the next day. Now he was a master at pacing himself, and could make a single draft last for an hour or more. He liked the stale smoky atmosphere of a drinking room, and he liked many of the men who came there. When Bryan could not reach his uncle at his new apartment, he had naturally tried the Rainbow Room.

"Jimmy, we've got to talk," Bryan said when he had zigged and zagged his way past empty tables.

"Hey, son, hang on a sec," the other dart player said. "Big point comin' here."

Jimmy took one look at his nephew, fired his dart and said, "See you, Mike. Your game. I'll settle with you tomorrow.

"What's wrong?" he asked Bryan. "You're soaked to the skin. Something happen with Iris?"

"No, not that. I've got to explain something, and it might take a while."

A few minutes later they were sitting at a quiet table. Bryan sipped the hot chocolate Jimmy had insisted on ordering for him and tried to put together all that had happened with the two so-called activist tree-hugger guests, then laid out his theory for Jimmy. When Bryan was finished, his uncle shook a cigarette from a crumpled pack. He blew the smoke toward the dark ceiling.

"You're right," he said at last. "It's the only explanation." He mashed his cigarette into the ashtray and stood up. "Let's go. We can put your bike in the back of the truck. I want to be there when they get home."

Bryan's uncle had a temper that was well known, although it hardly ever showed itself. Bryan had an uneasy feeling it was about to show itself that afternoon. "Shouldn't we tell Zeke?" he said.

"Sure, we'll tell Zeke. Right after I throw those two sonsabitches out of our house."

The longer they waited, the more Bryan began to question his wisdom in telling his uncle before he was able to contact Zeke. What if things get ugly? he thought, fidgeting. What can me and my one-armed uncle do against two big strong men who think nothing about lying and pretending, not to mention setting things on fire? What if they beat us both up? What if they come back some time and try to burn down the house?

He and Jimmy had come straight to their empty home. They prepared supper — which Bryan couldn't eat — and watched TV until after dark. As soon as he heard the basement door open and close, Jimmy hauled himself from the couch and headed for the stairs. Bryan followed, at a distance.

Through Otto's open door they could see both men, still in their rain jackets, talking. Jimmy didn't waste any time.

"You two fellas come out here. I want to talk to you."

Kevin/Kyle and Otto/Oliver slouched out of the bedroom, their faces curious. Otto stood more than a head taller than Jimmy. Kevin was bigger, too, and outweighed

Jimmy by at least twenty kilos.

Kevin turned on his smile and the syrupy charm. "Hi, Bryan. What's up?"

"You boys have fifteen minutes to get your gear together and clear out," Jimmy answered for his nephew.

Otto ran his fingers through black hair slicked down by the rain. "What the hell are you talking about? We've booked these rooms for another week, with an option to extend."

"Is there some sort of problem?" Kevin put in, his voice a lot less congenial.

"You might say that."

"Bryan," Kevin appealed again, his smile again. "Would you mind telling us what this is all about?"

The dark scowl that had flashed across Otto's face, and the physical threat that seeped from three angry men in a small space, intimidated Bryan and tangled up the words inside his head. He looked at his uncle. Jimmy's face was a rigid mask, made more threatening by the bruises, the livid scrape and the stitches.

"Leave him out of this," he snarled.

"We don't go without an explanation," Otto said through clenched teeth. "We've paid in advance. We —"

"We haven't been any trouble," Kevin said. "Have we, Bryan? No loud music, no parties, no women. Just like your mom asked. So, you have to understand, Mr. Lormer, we don't see — "

"We don't see," Otto cut in, "what this has to do with

you, anyway. We have an understanding with Iris, not you."

Bryan could feel the energy pulsing in waves from his uncle's body. Jimmy's chest heaved under his sling. "We don't need scum like you around here. I'm not gonna tell you again. Pack up and get out."

"Don't threaten me, you little —" Otto hissed, straight-arming Jimmy as he lunged forward.

As Otto's arm shot out Jimmy stepped quickly to the side, blocked the arm and, with the back of his fist, snapped a punch that made a sickening crack as it brought blood flowing from Otto's nose. Otto cursed, hand to his face. His eyes watered, and blood streamed between his fingers.

Kevin grimaced in anger. He swung, his round-house punch missing Jimmy's head and glancing off his shoulder as Jimmy twisted out of the way. He shoved Kevin back. Kevin let out a roar and wrapped his thick arms around Jimmy, trapping him in a bear hug. A snarl of pain crossed Jimmy's face as his broken arm was pressed between his own chest and the larger, heavier man. Jimmy drew back his head and butted. *Thunk*
! Kevin swore and fell back, an ugly red welt on his forehead. He gathered himself and attacked.

"Stop! I said stop, Kyle!" Otto shouted. Kevin stepped away, red faced, chest heaving. "Forget it," Otto said. "We'll go. There's lots of other places to stay in this ratty little town."

"I wouldn't count on it," Jimmy said.

"Oh, yeah —"

"Let it go, man," Otto ordered.

Jimmy stood his ground as they rapidly packed.

"The keys" was all he said as they were struggling out the door with their gear. Otto tossed two keys to the floor and slammed the door shut behind him. A moment later, their van roared to life and took them away.

Bryan's entire body shook as unused adrenalin surged through his muscles. He had not spoken or moved throughout the entire exchange. I was about as useful to my uncle as his maimed arm, he thought.

"So your uncle threw them out?"

"Did he ever! He stood right up —"

"Was there a fight?"

"Almost. One of them — Otto —"

"Almost? How can there be an almost fight?"

"Well, let me talk and I'll —"

"So talk."

When Bryan had finished the story, Ellen said, "So, can I say something now?"

"Sure."

"Somebody ought to put those two creeps in jail."

"Jimmy's going to call Zeke and tell him all about it."

"Good. Hey, I've got some almost good news."

"How can there be almost good news?"

"Very funny."

"Well?"

"My aunt might take me to visit your mom."

"Might?"

"Well, if it's okay with you."

"Sure it is. She'd be glad of the company."

"Great, Bry. My aunt wants to use the phone. Miss you. Bye."

While Jimmy talked to Zeke on the phone, Bryan ripped the linen from the beds and jammed it into the washing machine. After opening the windows wide, letting in the fresh damp night air, he vacuumed their rooms furiously. He wanted every trace of the two trouble-makers gone.

Jimmy was sipping a beer when Bryan finally went upstairs to the kitchen. "What did Zeke say?" he asked.

"You've been quite the detective, eh, Bry? Zeke told me you talked to him about those two donkeys before."

"Yeah. You know, when I think back on it, I felt kind of funny about those guys from the start."

"They were a little too good to be true, as far as I'm concerned," Jimmy agreed. "Anyway, they're gone."

"Thanks to you."

"Zeke told me he's going to pick them up tomorrow, at the peace camp. We agreed that's likely where they'll be."

"I'd like to be there when he does," Bryan said, "and see somebody get arrested who deserves it, for once."

Jimmy gave his nephew a look of surprise. "You don't think the protesters should get taken in by the cops?"

"I don't know what to think any more. Not just because my mom is one of them, either. I hate to admit it, Jimmy, but the first time Mom got arrested, I felt like she had it coming. Don't ever tell her I said that, okay? I'm not too proud about feeling that way. But when she was told she'd get six months, then I gradually changed my mind. And when I found out about the sabotage, and those two jerks you kicked out of here, I started thinking, what's going on here when people like my mother get thrown in jail for sitting on a bridge? I mean, okay, maybe people think she's wrong and being a pain in the neck for everybody — maybe I think that, too — but a thousand-buck fine? Six months in jail? For trying to get the government to protect our environment?"

Jimmy took a pull on his beer, frowning.

Bryan thought, Maybe I went too far, but Jimmy has always been the kind of person you can say what you want to. As long as you mean what you say, even if he thinks you're full of it, he respects you. That's the way he has always been. But now, his face was clouded.

Jimmy took out a cigarette and lit it with his big chrome-plated Zippo. "I'm with you," was all he said.

"Really? You changed your mind, too?"

"No, not about the logging. I'm a tree-cutter, Bry, and most of my friends are. It's what I've always been. But I've been thinking. There has to be a better way to work this out."

"Mom says there isn't. She says if people don't do something now, the government and MFI will stall for ages. Meanwhile, they keep clear-cutting."

"Yeah, well, between me and you, I've never been a

big fan of clear-cutting. There's other ways to harvest trees. I'll tell you what bothers me about this whole damn set-up though," Jimmy growled. "A bloody politician gets caught with his hand in the till, or gets nailed for what they call conflict of interest — which means he's using his position to make a lot of bucks — and they get a nice hearing at our expense, then sometimes, sometimes, they have to clear out. That's it. But my sister parks herself on a bridge in the backwoods of Vancouver Island and all of a sudden there's a keen interest in upholding the law. I never finished high school so I'm no great scholar, but even a dope like me can see that something stinks."

They were silent for a while, then Jimmy lit another cigarette. "I'm not so sure about this SAVE thing, either."

"Your new job? It's not working out?"

"Oh, I'm doing okay, I guess. It's early days yet. But last time I talked to Tanaka I asked him where all the money was coming from. I got to thinking about that big spread they laid on for that meeting you and me went to. And my pay. And the big operating budget Tanaka gave me. I had to wring it out of him — you noticed how smooth the guy is. He finally admitted that all the funding comes from MFI."

So much for ordinary people having a voice, Bryan mused.

"All I want to do is go back to work in the bush! Oh, well, nothing we can do." Jimmy sighed. "At least there's a good chance that Otto and Kevin will get sent up."

"That's not what Mom would say," Bryan murmured.

"Pardon, Bry?"

"Mom would never say 'There's nothing we can do.'"

Jimmy laughed. "You're right there, old buddy."

Later, when he was in bed, Bryan felt the burn of shame rush through him again. My girlfriend is taken away because of my family; I do nothing. Two frauds invade our house and use it as a base; I do nothing. If it hadn't been for Elias, we wouldn't have found out about them. When Jimmy was throwing them out, I just stood there. My uncle, one arm in a sling, took them both on and could have been beaten half to death, and I just stood by, watching.

My mother loses her job over something she believes in. And I criticize her.

Bryan lay in his bed, feeling like a straw man. And that was when he thought, if I can't throw Otto and Kevin in jail myself, I can be there when it happens.

# THIRTEEN

All night long the rain kept up a punishing tattoo on the roof, drumming Bryan from one nightmare to another. When his clock radio dragged him awake at six o'clock, he hauled himself out of bed and pulled on his clothing. After pouring down two glasses of orange juice, he grabbed a bagel from the fridge and left the house.

The morning was overcast, warm and muggy. The heavy air seemed to drag at him as he pedalled out of town, his bike tires hissing on the wet blacktop. He headed for the bush road that led to the peace camp and the Big Bear River, and by the time he made it he was soaked in sweat. He bumped along the road, breathing in the damp heavy smell of the sodden bush, a lush odour sharpened by the tang of spruce. Other smells greeted him as he emerged into the huge wasteland: smoke from the campfires, the homey scent of hot soup from the café, the weighty odour of decaying vegetation from the ravaged slopes that flanked the road.

Cycling through the camp, weaving among activists

and reporters, Bryan scanned the faces, searching for the two men he hoped to see behind the screened windows of a police van before the day was over. But Kevin and Otto were nowhere to be found. When he crested the hill that looked down to the bridge and the Big Bear, he stopped and surveyed the scene below him. Looks like I'm just in time to see some action, he thought.

The police van, three or four cruisers, a white compact with MFI painted in green on the door — all were parked at odd angles along the shoulder of the narrow dirt road. Just ahead of him, a knot of people blocked the way, lectured by a man with a megaphone. Three or four reporters, shouldering Betacams, panned the river valley. On the bridge, an eighteen-wheeler loaded with logs stood stationary, its engine grumbling over the rush of the river. Dwarfed by the big truck, a dozen seated figures silently dominated the scene. Except for the absence of yellow ribbons and counterprotesters, Bryan thought, things look pretty much like they did last time I was here. Well, more reporters, maybe.

Aware that he would get no farther along the crowded road, Bryan shoved his bike up the embankment, where he could get a better look at the goings-on. He pushed his bike into a thick wall of hemlock and spruce and then scanned the milling crowd — men, women, seniors, a middle-aged woman supporting herself with a cane. A few children. Some faces he recognized from town: a gallery owner; Mr. Gagnon, who taught phys. ed. at Bryan's school; a gas-station attendant. Bryan caught sight of Zeke balanced on the rear bumper of a cruiser. Zeke lifted a pair of binoculars to his eyes.

The electronic drone of the megaphone ceased, and the crowd, ebbing and flowing around the bridge the way shreds of mist float on the sea, took up the chant, "No more clear-cuts! Save Orca Sound!"

Bryan strained his eyes. There. Is it? Yeah, it's Elias! At the end of the bridge, beside the concrete railing, Bryan's friend stood draped in a torn poncho, a blue-and-white Toronto Maple Leafs cap on his head. He raised a placard, his lips moving. *Brazil of the North*, the sign read.

Bryan was stunned at finding sarcastic I-don't-give-a-damn Elias in the middle of a demonstration. Why didn't he tell me he was coming here, he thought, immediately knowing the answer. Because he knew I'd be against him. Bryan looked away. And that was the moment he saw Otto, right across from him on the other side of the road.

Bryan stepped back into the trees. Shielded by the wet skirts of a spruce, he watched. Otto was intent on the activity at the bridge. Bryan followed his line of sight and scrutinized the faces of those seated in front of the truck.

One of the protesters rose slowly until he stood with his back to the grille of the eighteen-wheeler. His wispy grey hair lifted in the gentle gusts that puffed through the noisy river valley. He crossed his arms on his chest and, looking neither right nor left, stood as immobile as a stump. Just the way he did the day they arrested my mother, Bryan thought. It was Walter.

As the chanting swelled around them, the bald man from MFI stepped up to the demonstrators. As he began to read, the crowd fell silent. When he finished, the voices rose again, more fervently. "No more clear-cuts! Save Orca Sound!"

Otto was still lurking just inside the edge of the trees. He bent down, busy with something at his feet. He stood straight. He had something in his hand. Bryan thought, it's a liquor bottle. And it's on fire!

Otto hurled the bottle toward the bridge. Then he disappeared into the trees.

"Walter! Elias!" Bryan screamed as a ball of orange flame exploded on the grille of the lumber truck and spilled over Walter's rigid form. He fell to the ground, engulfed in flames.

Bryan ran from the trees, stumbling down the embankment, plummeting full-length onto his face, rocks tearing his skin as he rolled onto the road. "Walter! Elias! Zeke! He's in the trees!" he screamed as he scrabbled to his feet and barged through the crowd. He fought his way to the bridge.

Pandemonium. Walter lying in the shallow water of the ditch, smoke rising from the burned clothing on his back. Elias kneeling beside him, slapping at Walter's burning shirt, his own hands blackened, his face creased and racked with pain. Voices shrieking "Police! Ambulance!" Lenses of video cameras poking through the wall of bodies surrounding Walter and Elias. Hands scratching at the road, hurling sand and dirt at the flames that engulfed the snout of the lumber truck.

Bryan Troupe, tears streaming down his face, useless. Once again.

# FOURTEEN

## *Victoria News Packet*

### EXTREMISTS CELEBRATE WITH MOLOTOV COCKTAIL

ORCA SOUND — In a move that a Mackenzie Forest Industries spokesperson called "inevitable," anti-logging extremists hurled a molotov cocktail — a bottle of flammable fluid using a rag as a fuse — at an MFI truck yesterday in a futile attempt to halt the legal harvest of trees in Orca Sound.

The incident occurred just as police were about to arrest more than 20 demonstrators blocking the Big River Bridge.

In motion since MFI was given the green light to begin the harvest in April, the daily demonstrations at the Big Bear River have lead to the arrests of more than 500 preservationists for defiance of an injunction prohibiting such actions.

Arsonists believed to be connected with the so-called Save Orca Sound organization have set fire to a truck, logging machinery and a trailer owned by MFI. "Luckily," said MFI spokeswoman Linda Hobbs, "nobody was in the trailer at the time. It could have been a disaster. This latest tragedy is part of the Green preservationists' campaign of violence."

# Vancouver Dispatch

## INJURED ACTIVISTS RELEASED

NOOTKA SOUND — CanNews — A Nootka First Nation man identified only as Walter and 15-year-old Elias Wilson, both of Nootka Harbour, were released from hospital today after treatment for burn injuries sustained when a fire-bomb went off during a demonstration near this resort community two days ago.

The older man, burned on the head, back and legs, left the hospital against the advice of doctors. Wilson suffered superficial burns to the hands and arms as he came to the aid of the older man when a molotov cocktail blew up during a peaceful anti-logging demonstration on the Big Bear River.

Police say one or both of the men may yet be arrested, as they were on the bridge in defiance of a court injunction acquired by MFI that forbids blocking the bridge or road leading to the logging site.

The demonstrations have been going on since the British Columbia government, which has recently purchased a large block of shares in Mackenzie Forest Industries, announced the Orca Sound Ecological Preservation Plan in April. The plan allows MFI to log two-thirds of the temperate rainforest around Orca Sound.

# *Victoria News Packet*

## TWO ARRESTED IN WAKE OF BOMBING

VANCOUVER — CanNews — Two men were apprehended yesterday in connection with a fire-bombing incident last week during an anti-logging demonstration on Vancouver Island.

Oliver McCann and Kyle Canning, both of Vancouver, were arrested as they left their North Vancouver rooming house by city police, who had been alerted by Nootka Harbour RCMP. At the time of their arrest, both men wore Save Orca Sound sweatshirts sporting Greenpeace buttons.

# Vancouver Dispatch

## "HUSH MONEY" LINKED TO MFI

VANCOUVER — Money was paid to two former North Pacific Forestry Alliance employees, Kyle Canning and Oliver McCann, arrested here two days ago, to deny their connection to the corporation, a former RCMP constable claims.

Ezekiel Wilson, lately of the Nootka Harbour detachment, presented evidence to city police alleging that, when they fire-bombed an MFI truck during an anti-logging demonstration on Vancouver Island two weeks ago, Canning and McCann were employed by NPFA as "ecological consultants." Wilson also charged that the two men are responsible for other acts of sabotage that destroyed unused equipment belonging to the company.

"They worked for NPFA," Wilson alleged, "and their job was simple — to destroy the credibility of the peaceful groups who organize the demonstrations against logging Orca Sound. After they were arrested they demanded, and got, money from Mackenzie Forest Industries to keep their mouths shut. They were represented by a lawyer from a firm retained by MFI."

Wilson is presently suspended without pay from the RCMP for conducting "unauthorized investigations."

MFI spokesperson Linda Hobbs, also a member of the board of North Pacific Forestry Alliance, claimed after the arrest of McCann and Canning that Wilson's "wild accusations" were prompted by revenge because his younger brother, Elias, a "typical activist hoodlum," was injured when McCann's fire-bomb exploded.

When information about the hush money came to light, Hobbs could not be reached for comment.

# Vancouver Dispatch

## LINK PROBED BETWEEN MFI AND NPFA

VANCOUVER — The North Pacific Forestry Alliance, which styles itself a moderate environmental organization dedicated to "taking a middle ground between extremist preservationists and the unfortunate practices of the forestry industry in the past, and promoting sustainable growth through preservation of the land base," is entirely funded by the forestry industry, the Dispatch has learned.

Set up in Vancouver five years ago, the Alliance's board of directors is drawn from Vancouver-area municipal politicians, academics and businesspeople — many of whom have ties to the industry.

In a move to counter a negative image that extended far beyond the borders of Canada into the U.S. and Europe, key players in the forestry industry hired the public relations firm Equivoc, which has made its reputation acting for multinational corporations at the root of ecological disasters ranging from oil spills off Alaska to chemical explosions as far away as India. Equivoc set up NPFA, and the chairperson of the board of NPFA, Nathan Epstein, is an Equivoc employee. Other key members of the board are hand-picked by Mackenzie Forest Industries.

Established to win the support of urban voters

for the industry, NPFA has produced two television documentaries, "The Forests and You" and "North Pacific, Land of Plenty," both of which defend clear-cut logging while at the same time arguing that the industry has changed its ways.

Epstein, when queried about the source of funding for NPFA, stated, "We operate at arm's length from the industry. Our view is entirely objective. The fact that the Alliance was set up by a public relations firm is entirely irrelevant." Asked about the recent arrest of Kyle Canning and Oliver McCann, both NPFA employees, and subsequent revelations about hush money paid to them by Mackenzie Forest Industries, Epstein said, "I've never heard of those men, and allegations of hush money are ridiculous."

# Vancouver Dispatch

## ENVIRONMENTALISTS CRITICIZE
## MFI "SWEET-HEART DEAL"

VANCOUVER — CanNews — Environmentalists all across Canada are outraged that the British Columbia government has bought a large block of shares in Mackenzie Forest Industries.

The purchase came to light weeks before the government's April announcement of the Orca Sound Ecological Preservation Plan, which allows

MFI to log two-thirds of the temperate rainforest around Orca Sound. Critics point out that the remaining one-third of the area is either beaches and swamps or was already preserved in parks.

Minister of Finance Charles Riker has said that the buy reflects "sound fiscal practice to which the government is dedicated and which was a major plank in the election platform."

"How can the government oversee a safe ecological use of our natural resources," Save Orca Sound spokesperson Iris Troupe asked, "when it profits from the misuse of our forests? How can the government police the company when the government is the company?"

Troupe spoke from the minimum-security jail in Nanaimo, where she is serving a 90-day sentence for contempt of court.

# FIFTEEN

For the third time, and with a curse even louder than on the first two tries, Elias dropped his hamburger. The halves of the bun parted and rolled onto the café table, leaving the mustard-slathered pattie and a limp slice of tomato resting on a bed of soggy fries-and-gravy.

"Dammit!" Elias hissed, earning a few stares from nearby diners.

"You said that already," Bryan pointed out, laying down a folded newspaper and biting into his chicken burger.

"Sure, make fun of an invalid, why don't you." Elias took up a fork in one heavily bandaged hand and, with an awkward stab, vengefully skewered the burger. Both arms were swathed in white from elbow to fingertips.

"You're not an invalid. An invalid would be home in bed. You're here, so that would make you, if anything, a valid."

"Valid, my butt. Ever since Ellen got you reading you've turned into a word snob. What's with the newspapers, anyway? How desperate are you for something to do?"

"Oh, I don't know. I've been sort of following the protests and stuff. Learned a lot, too."

"Next thing I know you'll want to move to the big city back east and ride the subway to work with a brief case in one hand and a newspaper in the other. Ouch!" Elias cried as he picked up his glass of root beer with his fingertips.

Bryan tapped the newspaper. "You and Walter are famous, now, eh? Zeke, too."

"Did they really quote your mother?"

"Yep."

"She's all right, your mom."

Bryan was beginning to think so, too.

"That was a great thing you did, Elias. Helping Walter like that."

"Yeah, well." Elias shrugged. "The cops didn't think so. They only decided yesterday, Zeke told me, not to charge Walter and me with contempt. And I wasn't even on the bridge. Or is it 'Walter and I'?" he added, smiling and shoving a french fry into his mouth.

Around them the midday crowd in Captain Ned's — a restaurant done up with nets that swooped from the ceiling and old broken crab traps hung on cedar-panelled walls — buzzed with conversation.

"I got a leave from my job at the park, did I tell you?"

"That's great. You know, it's funny," Bryan said. "You got hurt at the protest and your boss gave you a leave — which he should. Mom gets arrested, comes back to work the next day and gets fired. The whole town is split down the middle by all this."

"Yeah."

"Well, I'm glad Zeke is back on the job," Bryan said.

"He got the news this morning. He said they reinstated him but they gave him an official reprimand for investigating your former guests without permission. He may not stay too long, though. Zeke isn't so sure any more that he's cut out for cop work."

"He's one of the best ones we've got, if you ask me," Bryan said. "He's good at his work. What he did in Vancouver — on his days off — proved that. Even if it was unauthorized. They should praise him, not hassle him."

Outside, a summer storm darkened the sky and whipped up whitecaps on Gray's Passage.

"I don't know, Bry. Zeke says that what's happened since the spring has been pretty hard on him. He said he joined the force to catch bad guys, not throw his friends in jail."

During the weeks after the fire-bomb incident, Bryan had spent most of his time in an empty house. He talked to Ellen every day or so on the phone, but their conversations made him feel no better. He felt lonelier when he hung up than he had been before they began to talk. Iris phoned most mornings to ask him how he was getting along. "Fine," he'd report. "How about you?" "Fine," she'd answer. From there they had nothing to talk about.

Jimmy had quit his job at SAVE. "I just didn't feel right," he had told Bryan the night he moved back in. "I felt like a prostitute or something. Or a crooked used-car salesman. Calling people up and trying to get them to come to meetings. I'm not a telephone guy. I belong in the bush." Now he spent his mornings job-hunting in an empty landscape between those who hated loggers and those who supported an industry that had no work for him because he could not cut trees. His afternoons he passed in the Rainbow Room, honing the edge of his bitterness with cigarettes and beer.

Bryan's uncle was no longer the jovial childlike companion of Bryan's youth. Bryan's mother was still in jail, his girlfriend still in parent-imposed exile. Bandages and pain had rendered his friends helpless and suffering.

Not since the death of his father had Bryan felt so numb, as if he had been injected with a toxic drug that dulled his nerves and neutralized his emotions. Paralyzed, he floated like a ghost from room to room of the silent house, turning on the TV and clicking it off again almost immediately, leafing through magazines, reading over and over his books on whales, poring through the album of family photos from the days in Drumheller.

He took most of his meals with Walter, after preparing them on his neighbour's hotplate. Walter ate sitting in his broken rocker, wrapped in a shabby Hudson's Bay blanket, and soon after succumbed to the medication he was taking against the pain and infection of his burns. Bryan helped him to bed, fed Dog and returned home.

One day Walter commented over their breakfast coffee, "Guess them traps are pretty full by now," and for the first time Bryan took out the crab boat alone. He pulled up the traps, throwing the catch into wooden boxes and stacking the traps on the stern rather than bait and set them again. Then he returned the boat to Walter's slip and prepared it for a long period of disuse. With the money from the catch he bought groceries and put them away in the small cupboards in Walter's trailer.

That Sunday, Jimmy and Bryan drove to Nanaimo to see Iris, Sunday being the only day she was allowed visitors. Bryan had been looking forward to the trip, planning to visit Ellen for a few hours — until she told him over the phone that her parents were taking her to Vancouver that same day to see a play.

"They've had the tickets for ages, Bry. I can't get out of this!"

Iris appeared full of high spirits but, do what she would, she was unable to drag a smile to her son's lips. Misinterpreting Bryan's moroseness for anger at her, she tried to explain to him once again why she had allowed herself to be arrested the second time. The more she talked, the more pained the look on his face, so she gave up and said with false cheer, "I'll be home soon!"

"What home?" Bryan mumbled.

He could not tell her, because he could not put into words, that everything he loved and wanted was gone, and worse, it was not his mother who had deeply disappointed him.

# SIXTEEN

"You're too hard on yourself, Bry."

"Maybe. But I don't think so."

"Well, you are, but I'm not going to argue about it long-distance. So, what are you going to do today?"

"I don't know. Maybe sit out in the yard, catch some rays and read."

"Still devouring the newspapers, eh?"

"Yeah. Elias thinks I've gone mental. But I'm sort of hooked. The more I find out about this logging thing, the more I see that it's . . . well, *bigger* than the fight about Orca Sound. Mom and Walter are right, Ellen. But lovers shouldn't talk politics, right?"

"Right. Hey, how do you get four dinosaurs in a Honda Civic?"

"Dinosaurs are extinct. They've been gone for —"

"Okay, how do you get four extinct dinosaurs into an extinct Honda Civic?"

"Two in the front and two in the back."

"Aw, you've heard it."

"Yeah, Ellen, I fell out of my cradle laughing at that joke. I've heard every dinosaur joke in the book. I was born in the famous ditch, remember?"

"Want to have an obscene phone call, then?"

"Are you kidding? This is a law-abiding family. Didn't you know?"

"Right, right. Guess I forgot."

"I wish you were here, Ellen."

"Me, too, Bry. Something tells me you could use a hug."

"A hug, yeah. And —"

"You said you were law-abiding. I'm hanging up before you corrupt my ears. Talk to you tomorrow."

Saturday morning, after he had eaten breakfast with Walter, washed the dishes, fed Dog and tied him up outside, Bryan threw a couple of bottles of juice and three granola bars in his backpack and set off along the shoulder of the highway.

So that he would not encounter activists and demonstrators he had waited until Saturday to retrieve his bike, which, he hoped, was where he had left it on the embankment near the river. The logging trucks did not roll on the weekends, so the demonstrators used the time to rest up.

The sun was high when he reached the logging road that led to the Big Bear River. It was barricaded by a red-and-white log resting on two oil drums. An RCMP cruiser was parked on the shoulder of the highway. Bryan did not recognize the two cops who sat inside, smoking and talking. Probably got the air conditioning on, he thought, wiping the sweat from his brow and shifting the pack on his back. He hesitated for a moment, took a deep breath, and ducked under the barricade.

"Hey! Where do you think you're going?"

One of the cops was getting out of the car.

"I'm going to get my bike," Bryan said. "It's down by the river."

The cop shook his head. "This is a restricted area. The road's closed."

Bryan jammed his trembling hands into his pockets. "I thought this was a public road."

"I said it's closed," the cop answered firmly. "The premier is coming out here in a couple of days and we don't want any more trouble."

"I just want to get my bike. I'm not going to cause any trouble."

The cop pushed his cap back on his head and hitched up his belt, shifting his gun on his hip. "Sorry, son, you can't pass."

Bryan swallowed. "But this is public land. I can go where I want."

The cop waved a thick finger in Bryan's face. "Look, sonny, move off before you get into trouble."

Bryan's laugh brought a rush of scarlet to the big man's face. He gripped Bryan by the shoulder, turned him toward the cruiser and shoved. Bryan stumbled and grabbed the barrier. He ducked under the log and began to walk back along the highway.

"Trouble?" he mumbled to himself as he walked. As if he could give me more trouble than I've already got. I suppose the cops are going to throw people into the slammer for walking down the wrong road on a Saturday afternoon. Just because the premier's coming. Big deal.

On his way home, Bryan stopped at a milk store and bought a newspaper. He read the lead story as he walked.

## Victoria News Packet

### PREMIER TO CUT RIBBON

ORCA SOUND — Premier Charles Harrington will attend the official opening of Stage One of the Orca Sound Ecological Preservation Plan on Monday, the Premier's Office has announced.

Unveiled last April, the plan, which Harrington says "strikes a fair balance between rival positions held by environmentalists and forestry interests," allows Mackenzie Forest Industries to log two-thirds of the area. The remaining one-third will be protected, he said.

Orca Sound, one of the last relatively untouched temperate rainforests on earth, where several unique species of flora and fauna can still be found, has been the focus of demonstrations by environmentalists since MFI began logging there immediately after the announcement was made.

Activists claim Harrington's plan will make Vancouver Island the "Brazil of the North." More than 600 have been arrested for defying MFI's injunction against demonstrations.

The exact location of Premier Harrington's visit has not been announced.

Bryan read the rest of the paper at the kitchen table, munching reheated pizza. His thoughts kept coming back to the article about the premier's visit. That night, after Jimmy had gone to bed, Bryan set a fire in the fireplace, turned off all the lights and sat up late, feeding logs into the fire and staring into the flames.

The next morning, as usual, he went to Walter's trailer to cook him breakfast. When they had eaten, Bryan said, "Walter, there's something I have to do, and I need your help."

Walter nodded and waited. Bryan pulled a chair in front of the rocker and told his neighbour what he had decided the night before. When he had finished, Walter was silent. Bryan studied his craggy, weather-beaten face.

"Do you think I'm crazy, Walter?"

Walter put his hand on Bryan's shoulder. "I always knew," he said softly, "some day you were gonna understand what they were telling you."

"Who?" Bryan asked.

"The whales."

# SEVENTEEN

Bryan had lived in the Pacific Northwest long enough to know that he had to be prepared for all kinds of weather. He spent the rest of the morning assembling and packing his gear: rainwear, sleeping blanket, nylon fly; thick sweater; alarm clock (if he overslept, it would ruin everything), waterproof matches, toilet paper; sandwiches, granola bars, a thermos of coffee, a canteen of water; two large black felt-tip markers; Walter's compass and topographical map, which Bryan covered with plastic wrap; a length of lightweight chain and a combination lock.

He packed the gear in his room while Jimmy worked outside, brushing stain on one side of the house, a slow process for a man with one arm out of commission. Satisfied with his preparations, Bryan made sandwiches for Jimmy and himself, penned a brief note telling his uncle he was over at Elias's and would likely be there for the night, and slipped out of the house.

The midday sun was hot, the pack heavy and awkward, and by the time he made the docks Bryan was sweating. He stowed his pack in the bow of Walter's cedar skiff, which was tied up behind the crab boat. He unlocked the cabin and hauled out the outboard motor and gas tank, then locked the cabin again. Soon he was on his way down the channel of Gray's Passage, accompanied by the slap of waves against the hull and the cries of seabirds overhead. He steered the little boat southeast, holding course for more than an hour as the old outboard engine pushed him slowly past the month of Salmon Inlet, round the point of Big Bear Peninsula and then east into Big Bear Inlet.

Near its head the inlet began to narrow, and Bryan steered for the rickety dock on the north shore that Walter had told him about. One look at the rotten pilings and planks persuaded him to beach the boat rather than tie up to the old dock. He cut the motor and tilted it forward. When the bow scraped the rock shelf, Bryan scrambled over his pack and hopped out. He hauled the pack from the bow, then half lifted, half dragged the heavy skiff farther up the shelf. Lifting the motor from the transom, he lugged it to the fringe of evergreens. He hid the gas tank beside the motor and pulled the boat well up above the tide line.

Bryan pulled his map and compass from a pocket of the backpack, hung the compass around his neck and stuffed the folded map into his shirt pocket. He shouldered the pack and moved off up the shore until he reached the log cabin. At one time it had belonged to Walter's family; now, it was decrepit, the door gone, the cedar shakes rotten and mossy. Beside the building, an overgrown path struck north along the edge of the forest. Bryan followed it up away from the shore. A short walk, and he reached the snag that Walter had told him to look for — a bleached and weathered skeleton of a Sitka spruce poking far into the azure sky. At its tip, the afternoon sun picked out the white head of a bald eagle, serenely surveying the deep blue water of the inlet below.

Bryan drank from his canteen as he watched the majestic bird launch itself with a screech, unfurl its wide wings, beat its way upwards to soar in wide gyres above forest and sea. After the eagle had become a dot in the distance, Bryan took one last look at the sea in the direction of his house, took a bearing, and headed into the cool shade of the trees.

The rough terrain rose sharply, and soon Bryan was panting as he struggled over and around moss-blanketed deadfalls on legs beginning to ache from the strain. He stopped for a rest, leaning against a fir to support the weight of the pack. Slow down, he told himself, panting. You've got lots of time. "You're going to do this," he said out loud, "and you're going to do it right."

Setting off at a more moderate pace, he soon crested a ridge, grateful for the respite offered by the relatively flat land, and followed it for a while before his compass directed him down a gentle descent into a sun-filled glen, through waist-high ferns. As he entered the trees again he noticed that the forest was gradually changing. The trees that canopied the forest floor were taller, thicker, farther apart. He came to a creek that rushed away to the southeast — probably to join up with the Big Bear River, Bryan figured — twisting and turning through clumps of red alder, under moss-covered logs. By a large gravel bar that encircled the massive roots of a fallen red cedar, Bryan shucked off his backpack. He shook the last of the water from his canteen, refilled it in the stream, took a long drink so cold it numbed the back of his throat, and topped up the canteen.

Bryan sat on the sun-warmed gravel and took a long rest, eating granola bars and enjoying the afternoon sun that slanted through the bush. Birdsong trickled from branches. Squirrels scolded one another. The breeze sighed high in the treetops. Whoever, Bryan asked himself as he stood and shouldered his pack, came up with the idea that the forest was silent? He crossed the stream.

The terrain became rugged again. Bryan skirted swampy areas, struggled over rock outcroppings, climbed over fallen logs, constantly checking his compass, his only help as he slipped deeper and deeper into the forest. At the back of his mind, the itch of fear. He was not a woodsman; he could not read the forest the way Walter could. Would he become lost and wander for weeks until he starved? Trust the compass, Walter had told him back in the trailer. Don't trust your eyes or your sense of direction: for someone like you, they'll lead you around in circles. The compass will take you where the map shows. Trust the compass.

After several hours of rough trekking, Bryan found

himself in an old-growth forest, and the itch began to fade. Consulting his map once more, he nodded to himself, sighed heavily, and let his pack slide off his aching back. To the east, he could see the ground rise gently toward a ridge, the ridge that was a line on the map, the ridge Walter had told him to expect. Leaving his pack behind, he climbed the ridge and looked down on a road. He nodded to himself again and returned to his gear. He had made it.

Calmed, Bryan looked around. High above him, the early evening breeze moved through the treetops. He walked toward a colossal red cedar, then around it. The trunk was easily five metres in diameter — you could park a full-sized sedan on the stump, he mused — and soared like a living highrise almost a hundred metres above him. He stepped between the shoulder-high roots as if walking between two cars, and touched the thick shaggy bark, damp with moss and lichen.

Bryan knew from his Ellen-inspired reading that, when the Vikings pushed through North Atlantic storms and touched the prows of their galleys to the eastern shores of North America, this cedar was already old. It stood among Sitka spruce, each at least ninety metres high and three metres thick. They were already mature when John Cabot sailed from Bristol to begin explorations that eventually opened the Atlantic cod fishery. To him and his sailors, and to many generations after him, the shoals of cod must have seemed as inexhaustible as this forest. Now the cod were gone, the fishery shut down. Bryan turned slowly in a circle, examining the giant living beings that surrounded him. Soon after Cabot's era — a mere blink of time to these trees — Jacques Cartier sailed into the Gulf of St Lawrence and pierced the continent, looking for riches. They had all come looking for riches, Bryan thought, and believed they had found none.

Standing there in awe, Bryan understood now why Elias's father filled canvas after canvas with images of these living pillars and the animals that moved among them; why Walter believed the spirits of his ancestors walked here. And why his mother — despite Bryan's opposition — had chosen jail rather than do nothing while these ancient trees fell to the loggers, for she knew that, once felled, they would be gone forever. At one time indifferent to their presence, Bryan now shuddered at the thought of chain saws spewing sawdust as they ripped through the growth rings of these giants; of clamorous machines snorting diesel smoke, grinding ferns and seedlings under huge tires as they dragged away the corpses of the trees, leaving slash and waste behind like the bones of extinct animals to rot in ground that had not felt the unfiltered heat of the sun since long before Jesus entered Jerusalem.

As the light rose higher in the trees, Bryan set up his camp. He tied two corners of the nylon fly to young hemlocks springing from a decaying deadfall and pinned the other end to the ground with sticks. After placing a waterproof sheet on the ground under the fly, he spread his sleeping blanket and set his alarm clock.

In the chill of the evening he ate his sandwiches, washing them down with hot coffee. Then he crawled under the fly, undressed and rolled his clothes to make a pillow. He tucked himself in his blanket and closed his eyes. He had walked a long way, packing a heavy weight, and he was tired.

# EIGHTEEN

At exactly ten o'clock in the morning the *whok-whok-whok* of an approaching helicopter beat the treetops east of the Talbot Inlet airport. A few minutes later, the aircraft gently descended from a clear blue sky, coming to rest some distance from the terminal building. A white stretch limousine drew up as three men and a woman deplaned, shoulders hunched against the turbulence of the blades. Clutching his cap firmly to his head, the chauffeur opened the limo's rear door. Before the helicopter's blades came to a stop, the limo had swept away, escorted by two police cruisers.

In the car with Premier Harrington were his two aides and Linda Hobbs, spokesperson for Mackenzie Forest Industries and organizer of the event.

"Nice here, eh?" Aide Two offered as the limo whispered along the highway. The last of the morning mist hung in the upper branches of the conifers that lined the road.

"Where are the reporters?" the premier demanded.

"What good is a photo-op without reporters?" He glanced at his gold Rolex.

"No sweat, boss. They'll meet us *en route*," replied Aide One, crossing his legs and brushing a speck of lint from his lapel. "There they are now," he said after some time had passed.

The limousine came to a halt at a side road from which two RCMP constables were removing a red-and-white log barrier. Parked at the side of the highway were three sedans full of reporters as well as a TV news minivan. The limo moved off again, trailing the police car along the road into the clear-cut area. Another cruiser slipped in behind the limo.

"This is the gathering place of the activists," Aide Two pointed out. "There's the so-called Rainforest Café."

"Why weren't those signs taken down?" was the premier's response. "For chrissakes, Ben, that's all we need!"

"Linda, I thought you said the area was secure," Aide One said.

"Sorry," the flustered woman answered.

Reporters were snapping photos of the *Orca Sound, Not Clear-Cut Sound* sign, while the TV man trained his Betacam on a poster that shouted in blood-red letters: *B.C. Chainsaw Massacre*.

"Too late now," Aide Two said philosophically. "Besides, maybe we can turn this around on them."

"Sure," the premier muttered, glancing at Hobbs, who was making notes with a gold fountain pen.

The limo floated sedately over the uneven logging road and re-entered the trees. As it descended the hill, Ben pointed ahead through the windshield. "There's the river, sir. The logging site is over the bridge and just on the other side of that hill."

"You have my speech?"

Ben patted his pocket. "It's right here."

"Hey!" Aide Two cut in. "What's that on the bridge?"

The Big Bear River valley had dressed up in its finest for the premier's visit. Morning mist swirled and danced on the surface of the swiftly flowing water, gracefully rising, illuminated by slanting gold bars of sun, slipping among the thick green branches of the spruce and firs that lined the road. Above, a dome of blue sky. Ravens cawed. A bald eagle circled on the updrafts of warming air.

The limo had come to a halt and its rear doors hung open. Aides One and Two stood on one side of the car, the premier and MFI's spokesperson on the other. Below them, the drifting mist swirled around the bridge. All eight eyes were trained on the large yellow patch.

"There's words on it," Ben announced.

"Words?" The premier squinted. AV HE EES, he read. A light breeze stirred the mist. The sun illuminated, briefly, the yellow sign. Yes, he could see clearly now. He could make out the words. "Get on the phone!" he shouted. "Get the cops!"

When the three sedans slid in unison to an abrupt halt

in the middle of the dirt logging road, all the reporters piled out, hollering, and ran toward the bridge. Unprepared for such a hasty stop, the TV van swerved around the reporters' empty cars and roared downhill, careered alongside the police cruiser and, with a sickening shriek, ripped off the driver's door. With all four wheels locked up, the van slid broadside, tearing up dirt and stones before it clipped the left rear fender of the pristine limo, shattering the tail light and coming to a stop in a cloud of dust, half in the ditch, blocking the road. The side door crashed open and, with a wireless microphone in her hand, a woman jumped out, followed by a young man with a Betacam. Without so much as a glance at the carnage caused by the van, they ran downhill.

The premier stood helpless, swatting dust from his suit as the melee swirled around him. Ben shouted into the car phone; Aide Two remained fixed to the spot, his mouth opening and closing like a bewildered bass. Linda Hobbs shook her head, capped her pen and got back in the car.

In the distance, sirens. At the bridge, cameras whirred as reporters snapped pictures. Cellular phones appeared and writers read from hastily scribbled notes. Framed by the Betacam, the TV woman buttoned her orange blazer and began to talk into the mike.

The camera operator began with Megan, medium close-up, then zoomed back to take in the yellow nylon tent fly lashed between the bridge abutment and a massive cedar stump, fluttering in the breeze, intermittently revealing the words SAVE THE TREES. As Megan spoke, the camera panned to the spectacle on the bridge. Zoom in on the boy who sat on a blue backpack, dead centre in the middle of the bridge, a thermos beside him. Zoom out to take in the entire bridge again. Pan left to the concrete railing, where a chain was doubled around one of the uprights. Tight shot of the chain, hardware-store variety, lightweight. Pan right, tight on the chain, following it to the boy's chest, where it encircled him, secured by a combination lock. Follow the chain, slowly, to the right side of the bridge, secured to a concrete upright. Zoom out to establish the scene again, reporters and cops milling around. Medium close-up of Megan as she winds up.

"Megan Sutton, CBC News, Orca Sound. That's a wrap," she added, lowering the mike. "Where's Harrington? He's next."

Although by now the sun was high enough to burn off the remains of the morning mist and flood warmth over the treetops and into the river valley, Bryan trembled. He tucked his hands in his armpits, the chain cold on his fingers.

Earlier the insistent *beep! beep!* of his alarm clock had wakened him to the rich damp odours of the forest and the drip of moisture on the fly above him. Quickly he had pulled on his clammy clothes and, as the morning light crept down the trunks of the spruce that stood around him like giant sentinels, he packed up his gear. After gulping down a cup of lukewarm coffee — he was too nervous to eat — he had set off. Through the chilly ground mist he hiked up the ridge, followed it for a few hundred metres and descended to break out of the trees and onto the logging road. The entire river valley was filled with fog as thick as cream. Behind it he heard the Big Bear rushing to the sea.

While invisible ravens squabbled in the trees around him, Bryan had spread the yellow fly on the ground and printed his sign. The black ink had bled into the wet nylon, but the letters were big and easily visible. It had taken just a few moments to set up the sign and the chains. While he waited he sipped the tepid coffee and rehearsed in his mind what he would do, psyching himself up for the confrontation that he knew would probably terrify him. When he had heard the sound of motors, he had locked himself in.

Bryan had not known what to expect, but never would he have imagined the chaos before him, cars and people everywhere. The moan of sirens swelled to a climax, then abruptly died when two more police cars arrived.

Bryan shut his eyes against the incessant flashing of cameras. It seemed the reporters couldn't get enough pictures of him. He ignored the questions they shouted at him.

"What's your name?"

"Are you part of a bigger protest?"

"Where do you go to school?"

"How old are you?"

"Who put you up to this?"

"Where are the rest of them?"

He looked at the ground when the TV man trained the Betacam on him.

Bryan felt like the only sane person in a lunatic asylum.

To no one in particular the premier shouted, "This is a goddamn fiasco!" To the cops he snarled, "Couldn't you even control a logging road? Isn't that your *job*?" To Aide One: "Ben, get the car turned around!" To Linda Hobbs: "Get out of the car. Here comes that bitch from CBC!"

"We can't move," Ben said. "The van's blocking the car."

"I'll need to fill out an accident report on that van," one of the cops said.

"Premier Harrington, would you care to make a statement?" asked the TV reporter icily. She had apparently heard the premier's description of her.

"Get her out of here," demanded the premier. "Why the hell haven't they arrested that little creep on the bridge?"

"The premier is not," Aide One said evenly, "prepared to make a statement at this time."

Undeterred, the newswoman stepped closer to the limo. She buttoned her blazer. "Premier Harrington, I'm going on record in ten seconds." She turned to her camera operator. "Ned, get ready."

Aide Two grabbed her arm. "Move out, Megan. You heard the prem —"

The reporter called, "Ned, are you rolling? Let go, buddy, or I'll charge you with assault. Premier Harrington," she said into her mike as the aide quickly released her, "what is the reason for such heavy security on this public bush road this morning?"

The premier drew himself up. His face became a mask of calm reasonableness, lit by a broad smile. "The Orca Sound Ecological Preservation Plan is a fair compromise between the demands of environmental activists and legitimate forestry management." He gave the self-deprecating shrug for which he was famous. "I am fully aware," he continued, his voice heavy with sincerity, "that this plan will not satisfy the more . . . ah . . . vociferous elements on either side of the issue. But the government thinks that this compromise is a fair and reasonable one that will create thousands of jobs and add to the prosperity of all citizens in our beautiful province."

"If the plan is fair, Premier, why have more than six hundred people been arrested trying to oppose it?"

Harrington's face became serious. "If people break the law, they must be prepared to take the consequences. Vigilante actions have no place in this country."

"Does that mean you are in agreement with what many across Canada feel are overly punitive sentences handed down by the courts?"

"It would be inappropriate for me to comment on

decisions made by our learned and hard-working judges. Now, if you'll excuse me —"

The reporter lowered the mike. "Thank you, Mr. Premier," she said stiffly.

"Why isn't that little sonofabitch arrested yet?" Harrington screamed.

"Megan Sutton, CBC News, Orca Sound." She had lowered her mike but hadn't switched it off.

Inside the Betacam, the tape rolled.

Bryan felt the cold clutch of fear as three RCMP officers approached him — a sergeant and two constables. One of the cops carried a pair of bolt cutters. The other was Zeke Wilson.

Bryan stared at the six shiny black boots in front of him, the six navy blue legs, each with a broad yellow stripe down the outside. Swallowing on a dry throat, he looked up at three navy blue bomber jackets and three stern faces.

"What's your name, son?" the sergeant asked.

Bryan looked through the legs at the reporters who had formed a semicircle behind the cops. Cameras clicked. Pens flew across steno pads.

"I asked your name, son." When he got no reply the sergeant said, "Either of you two officers know this lad?"

"His name is Bryan Troupe." It was Zeke.

Bryan looked up at him. Anger clouded Zeke's dark face, filling Bryan with doubt and a deep loneliness. He pressed his eyes closed, determined to control himself and his fear.

Hooking his thick thumbs in his belt, the sergeant demanded, "What's the combination to that lock?"

Bryan looked at his hands, fingers linked together in his lap, knuckles white. He took a deep breath and fought to control his voice. "I forget."

Sensing something, the reporters pressed closer. The man with the Betacam stood to the side; the tiny red light on the front of the camera glowed.

"Constable Briggs, move those reporters back," the sergeant growled. A shuffle of feet followed. "Now, son, I don't know if you realize the seriousness of what you're about here, but I want you to undo that lock. What's the combination?"

"I forget."

"All right, son, we'll play it out your way. Constable Wilson, place this young man under arrest."

"No."

Bryan's frightened eyes snapped up to Zeke's face, and his heart soared as he realized that Zeke's anger was not directed at him.

The sergeant glared at Zeke but directed his order to the other cop. "Briggs, cut the boy loose."

"Yessir." The chain to Bryan's left parted in the jaws of the bolt cutters and clinked to the ground. Moving behind him, the constable cut the chain on Bryan's right. The cop stepped back. Bryan remained where he was.

"Wilson, do your duty," the sergeant commanded.

"My duty, Sergeant, as I see it, does not include

arresting a fifteen-year-old boy for sitting on a bridge."

"Then stand aside. I'll deal with you later. Briggs, put the lad under arrest."

The second constable crouched in front of Bryan, who now recognized him as the cop who had refused to let him past the barrier to fetch his bike. The cop pushed his cap back. His voice was almost gentle as he spoke.

"Bryan Troupe, I am arresting you for violation of a legal court injunction which forbids the blocking of this road. Do you understand?"

Bryan was aware of the breeze on his face, the weight of the chain around his chest. He looked past the constable's shoulders at the reporters, then at the cedar stump, and his mind went back over the Rockies and the prairie to his old home in Drumheller, where the bones of extinct dinosaurs lay in the dry sands of the Badlands. He thought then of the whales, and he looked the constable in the face.

"Yes," he said. "I understand."

# EPILOGUE

In the weeks that followed the first arrest of Bryan Troupe at the bridge over the Big Bear River, daily protests against the clear-cut logging at Orca Sound continued. Among those charged for defying MFI's court injunction were Elias Wilson, Walter, Zeke Wilson and, the day after her return to Nootka Harbour, Ellen Thomson.

By the end of the summer, the number of men, women and children arrested had risen to seven hundred.

# ACKNOWLEDGEMENTS

Thanks to John Pearce and Ting-xing Ye for support and encouragement in the writing of this book.